V

The Complete Vampire in Vegas Trilogy
S.C. Principale

Vampire in Vegas : Complete Trilogy
Copyright © 2020 by S.C. Principale
All rights reserved. Printed in the United States of America. No part of this book may be used or reproduced in any manner whatsoever without written permission except in the case of brief quotations embodied in critical articles or reviews.

This book is a work of fiction. Names, characters, businesses, organizations, places, events and incidents either are the product of the author's imagination or are used fictitiously. Any resemblance to actual persons, living or dead, events, or locales is entirely coincidental.

For information contact:
https://scprincipale.wixsite.com/website
https://www.facebook.com/WritesandBites

Book and Cover design by Designer : S.C. Principale using public domain, free-for-use, free-to-alter, no attribution required images.

First Edition : 02/2020

Dedication:

To my incredible husband, who makes writing happy endings a matter of personal experience.

To my writing family : Judy, Rachelle, Katherine, Kathleen, Hebi, Sofia, Lois, Terry, Michelle, Dawn, Jen, Susan, Annee, and so many more.

ALSO BY S.C. PRINCIPALE

Contemporary Romance/Romantic Suspense
Passion: Sisters of Sin Femme Fatale Series[1]
Repairs[2]
Turning the Tables[3]
It's Business, Baby: Mature, Curvy Erotic Romance[4]
The Lady of the House: Mature, Curvy Erotic Romance[5]
Chocolate Krinkles and Two Kris Kringles[6]
Belgravia Security: A Bodyguard Romance[7]

Paranormal Romance
Pale Girl[8]
CrossRealms: You an' Me Against the World[9]
CrossRealms: Healing Hope[10]

1. http://books2read.com/u/3n5DX6
2. http://books2read.com/u/br1oVZ
3. https://books2read.com/u/mv1R18
4. http://books2read.com/u/bPyG07
5. http://books2read.com/u/4jPooD
6. http://books2read.com/u/mVRwkJ
7. https://www.amazon.com/Belgravia-Security-A-Bodyguard-Romance/dp/B09DDHWF3C
8. http://books2read.com/u/bPQ0aJ
9. http://books2read.com/u/bwKrvP

CrossRealms: Gestures[11]
CrossRealms: A Helpful Gentleman[12]
CrossRealms: Wicked Woods[13]
CrossRealms: Shattered[14]
CrossRealms: Mended[15]
CrossRealms: Whole[16]
Mountain Bound: A Monstrous Love Story[17]
Vampire in Vegas[18]

Historical Romance
Alliance[19]

---

10. http://books2read.com/u/4ApQoK

11. https://books2read.com/u/mlAJJA

12. https://books2read.com/u/3kPnER

13. http://books2read.com/u/m0B8GA

14. https://books2read.com/u/mBwEev

15. https://books2read.com/u/baDAPa

16. https://books2read.com/u/mKpo9d

17. http://books2read.com/u/bPQp6A

18. https://books2read.com/u/menE09

19. https://www.amazon.com/kindle-vella/story/B0B4F2RB94

Vegas is wild. A vampire in Vegas? Even wilder.

CHARLOTTE IS AN AVERAGE girl. She goes to NYU Pine Ridge, she loves her mother, is obsessively close to her best friend, Tessa, and has a stupidly hot boyfriend, Robert, who would kill for her (literally).

No one can believe that Charlotte talked quiet, shy Tessa and their musician boyfriends into heading to Vegas for a birthday vacation.

Two young couples seeing Vegas? Perfectly normal. The couples themselves? Not so much.

A quartet of friends will find their unique abilities give them a new, passionate twist to the old saying, "What happens in Vegas, stays in Vegas."

Get ready for a spicy erotic romance with a paranormal twist...

From Vampire in Vegas

I imagined. Leo's arm in Robbie's mouth, Tessa rubbing his chest as I nibbled Robbie's ear, loving the purring noise he makes as he drinks. Watching two erections strain against jeans.

Watching Leo suddenly push Tessa to the floor and shove her skirt over her hips as Robbie dragged me into his lap and unzipped, cock on display right before it sheathed in me.

Knowing they were watching.

Knowing we were watching them.

Vampire In Vegas

Part One

I love Pine Ridge. It's one of the prettiest towns in upstate New York. It has the best maple-glazed donuts in the world, one heck of a minor league hockey team (Go Lumberjacks!) and the taxes are startlingly low.

That could have something to do with its location on a Ley Line. Multiple Ley Lines. Three, to be exact, and they're all dark ones. In other words, Pine Ridge is pretty evil.

Not the people! Don't get me wrong, the people are lovely. Mostly. But it's not unusual to find a vampire, werewolf, or a succubus just trying to blend in. They can exist near dark magic. Some feed on it too heavily and blending in goes out the window. It turns into slaughtering and there goes the neighborhood. That's where I come in.

Charlotte. Blonde hair, blue eyes, 5'4", and one-quarter demon on my daddy's side. He was a great guy, but not really into commitment. That sucked for my mom, who had to raise me pretty much alone. It also sucked, because she never realized that her little girl wasn't just "freakishly" fast and strong growing up, I was supernaturally fast and strong. And I could see demons. Bad ones. Good ones. Demons who look like humans. Completely human humans, who just have power.

All demons have that ability. It helps them find victims- or allies.

Even when I was a kid myself, I knew there was something special about the little girl down the street. I could see a golden glow buzzing around her skin. I knew Tessa was powerful before she ever realized it. Tessa is a witch, all-human, and all-brain. She can't see what I can see, but she's too smart to let fear rule her head. She started dating Leo during her junior year of high school. He got bitten by a werewolf during his freshman year of college. A lot of girls would have freaked and loaded up the silver bullets. She just told him he has to sleep in his own reinforced, steel-padlocked, silver-lined room for three nights of the month.

They're going to get old and gray together, those two. (He's already kind of gray sometimes. And shaggy. I told her it's like a two for one deal- boyfriend and pet! She didn't laugh.)

I'm happy for them. Robbie and I are just as in love, but we won't have the same happy ending. I'll get old. He won't.

It's hard to get old once you're undead.

Robbie Scarsdale is Photoshop gorgeous with dark hair, blue-green eyes, one dimple, and lips and eyebrows that are in sinful partnership together every time he looks at you. He was always like that, before the whole "undead" thing. I thought he was poster-worthy the second I saw him— a new transfer student at Pine Ridge High after he and his uptight uncle moved over from London after his mother passed away. Robbie has been my other best friend since the day I spilled my lunch on him during our sophomore year.

He's been a vampire since his sophomore year of college. The cancer that took his mother was hereditary. It was also inoperable. In any other city in the world, you die or you get eaten. In Pine Ridge, you find one of the vampires who want a quiet life and who is willing to do a favor for a neighbor. Now, Robbie stays young and pretty. I get old. Possibly ugly. Boring?

Robbie doesn't think so. He's in love. I'm in love. But I won't last...

I don't want to think about it.

Vegas, anyone?

"I GOT A NIGHT FLIGHT. If we have delays or cancellations or a window seat, don't worry. I can cast a protective cloaking spell around Robert. Now, I have my carry-on, Leo's checking the bags, our tickets are—"

"Tessa! Breathe." I hold my best friend's hand. She's never flown on a plane. She'll be 21 in three days, but she's never flown on a plane. Oh well, her parents are still together, so she didn't have to fly between New York and Florida every summer.

"One day, Skin Deep will be headlining Vegas," Robbie sighs happily as he and Leo return from the baggage check via the snack bar. Skin Deep is the band they're in. If you couldn't guess, the name has a hidden meaning for a couple of the members who appear human but have a little extra.

"Yep." Leo doesn't talk too much, which is okay because Tessa talks enough for seven. Ordinarily. Right now, she's gone into pale and quiet "about to puke" mode. Leo pulls her to a corner, auburn hair tangling with her fire-red to whisper something and take deep breaths. She starts to smile again. I start to smile. I start to get all misty and then—

Cool hands on my arms, the back of my neck, lifting my hair. "You hungry?"

"Happy early birthday, Baby," his London drawl tickles my ear, and something colder tickles my neck. A gold necklace with a big emerald set in tiny diamonds drapes over my throat. I recognize it from every picture I've ever seen of his mother.

"Robbie!" I gasp and whirl. "You can't give me your mother's-"

"She told me to give it to my wife. That's you, init? In the future?"

"Robbie..." We talk about this. He talks about this. I change the subject.

"We'll get married in the little chapel at Pine Ridge Non-Denom. Moonlight ceremony. I'll get you a ring- once Bertie and I pay off the bloody uni loan people. Talk about demons..."

"We can't-"

"You're my captive audience on a four-hour flight, Sweetheart. How many times are you gonna ask me if I want peanuts?" To that end, we know it's hard to feed a vampire safely on a flight. Robbie doesn't kill. He gives me the occasional love bite and he and the butcher have a thing, and the local deer hunters think he's the best shot they've ever seen. Right now, he has a silvery juice pouch and a straw.

It ain't Capri Sun in there.

"I'm going to get old. I'm going to die."

"Or... when you want to try the liquid diet, I bite you in a new way. No pressure. I don't care if you live out your natural life and get old. Tessa can age me up with a spell. I can be your hunky boy toy in the nursing home."

"Dear God, please stop." The thought of Mr. Gorgeous making out with an eighty-something me, complete with wrinkles and false teeth, is enough to make me gag.

"Please stop what?" Tessa is back, very perky and less pale.

"Giving her my literally undying love," he sighs dramatically.

"Engagement gift?" Leo jerks his square jaw toward my neck, sandy eyebrows arching ever so slightly. Again, not big on the words, but huge on brains, just like Tessa.

"Absolutely," Robbie says as I murmur, "Not quite."

"Work it out, man. We have the same suite."

"We're not fighting," I'm quick to reassure everyone, even myself. "I just don't... know how all of this would work. When one half of a couple is going to age and die and the other... isn't."

"Well," Leo looks around and then continues in a furtive voice, "you're not going to age like the rest of the world. You're part demon."

"Your cells break down and replenish differently. I'd say, given your current metabolic level and the speed and strength I see you exhibit... Maybe you'll age half as slowly as most humans now that you've reached maturity?" Tessa says all this casually like she's telling me about a new ice cream place to try. That's the bio-med major in her. It comes so freaking easy for Tessa and Leo, while Robbie and I, two English majors, just nod and shrug.

"So you'll look forty when you're eighty. I'll still look in my rugged 20s, but that's not unheard of. It'll be fine, Lottie, you'll see." His fingers slip between mine. "Don't you know death doesn't have a watch, Sweetheart?"

That sounds like a song lyric. In fact, it might be one of their song lyrics. I should know that. Bad girlfriend, here.

This time, I'm being led into a corner, and Tessa and Leo stand by the rows of bolted-down chairs, watching planes taxi in and lift off.

Robbie's cool, slender fingers stroke my cheeks as our eyes meet. I ignore the crackle of speakers and the whoosh of planes, mesmerized by his voice.

"I almost died last year. Mum died when she was 38. If this plane goes down, not even being undead will save me from dying. Don't you see? I'm gonna die anyway, one day, and so are you. We oughta be together as much as we can, now. Don't say no anymore. Promise?"

I've never said a flat no. I've put it off. I've pushed it away.

I'm an idiot. I remember when they said that horrible word "cancer" followed by "inoperable", later followed by "not responding to radiation or chemo." I remember all those things and forget that our time might be short or uneven. It was almost over.

"I love you. I promise I won't say no. But maybe... maybe we don't have to talk about it this weekend?"

"Deal. Kiss on it?"

He's so corny. He's a corny, hot, English major who plays guitar. I mean, you take out the fangs and the chilly fingers and he's every girl's dream. And I get to keep him for my whole life, as long or short as that is.

"Kiss on it."

YOU CAN GET A CAR AT any time of night in Vegas. The hotel has a shuttle. Robbie and Leo sprang for this trip, and they went all out. Leo and Tessa's families are two-parent, high-earning types. They both got free rides to any university in the states, and some in Europe, too. They stick in Pine Ridge because it's easier to deal with witchy and wolfy issues. The point is, Robbie and I know that they are being way too generous with this four-star palatial hotel right on the strip, and we love them for it.

Loudly.

"This place is fucking hardcore luxury!" Robbie, who is just barely six feet tall, is carrying Leo around on his back. Leo is a couple of inches shorter than him and covered in long, lean lupine-esque muscle, howls and cracks open two beers. He's twenty-one already. Robbie would be, if… yeah. Do you have birthdays when you're undead? I think you do, at least in Pine Ridge.

With that supernatural strength, Robbie grabs up Tessa, too. "Look at me, Babes, I'm the strong man in the circus! Get a pic, get a pic!"

The first photo of our vacation is Tessa perched on his left shoulder, Leo draped across his back, and Robbie toasting me with a can of something cold.

I love these people so much.

Especially the one in the middle.

And now I'm aching in the middle. That hot, tight, slick sort of ache that screams for something thick, long, and cold.

Not an ice cream cone.

Robbie's blue-green eyes flicker. You can see, if you look carefully, a sudden crimson tint underneath. Some vamps have blood lust, and you see their canines slip down, long and pearly, the eyes turn red, and something— an overall something under the surface slicks back in them, making them look more lethal and sharper.

Robbie has lust right now. Just the ordinary, "I want my girlfriend" kind. He says he can smell the shift in hormones, smell the wetness, and hear the heart start to race with desire.

Leo tugs Tessa down with his usual lack of discussion. With way more openness than I'm used to, he backs her against the wall and kisses her hard, mouth open, hands pulling her waist to his. His hands tighten on her body, then her hair, pulling back to let her breathe.

I should not get so wet watching my best friends kiss.

But...

"Nap?" Leo asks.

"Okay!" Tessa squeaks. "I think I have jet lag," she says lamely, bust heaving.

"We'll go out." Vegas at nighttime is at its best, according to what everyone says, but also because, duh, sunlight-challenged boyfriend. I want to go explore our bedroom, but it wouldn't be fair to Robbie.

Robbie, who is herding me toward our door of the suite. "Me, too, Tess. Exhausted."

"What are we going to do all day?" I offer a feeble protest.

Leo stops, panting slightly, hand sliding up Tessa's ribcage, lifting her pink shirt to reveal perfectly creamy, rose-kissed skin. "I think we can think of something to do together. Or separately."

Like two wolves that hunt together, in the same pack but with different mothers, Leo and Robbie seem to understand each other. Leo sniffs in, chin raised slightly. He does something behind Tessa that makes her gasp, head arching back.

Robbie's erection is going to tear through my jeans, it's so hard. I look over my shoulder. Fangs are down, eyes are done hiding their scarlet depths. "Yeah. We'll work it out. Together or separately."

He all but shoves me through the door and clings to me as I lock it. "Are you okay?"

His face has reverted. He's fine —enough. "Leo knows. Shit."

See, it's the depth of my love and the basis of best friends here that prevent me from thinking horrible things. Things like Robbie wants Tessa. Robbie and Leo want to sleep with Tessa.

My stupid voice is just a little slow on the uptake. "What? What does he know?"

"He gets it. The craving. He can eat raw meat three times a month, hunt in the forests where I take him, as long as I go with him."

"I'm not—"

"Sweetheart, I'm not evil. I'd never, ever kill. I don't want to."

"Huh?" What the hell is happening?

"But... sometimes, tasting a different flavor is tempting. I can't ask anyone but you. I love you so much." He presses me close again, desperately seeking my eyes, looking so guilty. "No wonder you don't want to marry a —"

"Robert! Stop!" I yank his forehead to mine. See, I know I'm in love enough to marry this guy because I find his red eyes pretty. Like rubies. I love his pointy teeth and when he smiles and laughs with them on, I find it sexy, not scary. Because it's him. "I do want to marry you. I don't think you're smart for wanting to marry me, but..."

"What did you say?"

Why am I suddenly so tall? Oh.

Robbie's whirling me above his head, ala Cinderella and the Prince, bringing me down into a back-bending kiss. "Yes, I want to marry you, goofball," I pant, pushing him off. He needs air to speak. Not to breathe. Sometimes he forgets my requirements are a little different. "But not if you have some secret urge to bang my best friends." The keyword was secret. When I saw Leo and Tessa... I don't want to join in, but I found myself guiltily realizing that I wouldn't mind watching a little bit. I mean, a little. If they were okay. Argh.

Vegas has some sort of moral magnetic forcefield. That's what it is.

Robbie dropped me, arms suddenly limp. Fortunately, he dropped me over the bed and this mattress is made of marshmallows wrapped in silky smooth fabric.

Being stranded in our suite during daylight hours would be awesome. Not that Robbie couldn't move around from place to place if he stayed in the shadows, but we try not to take risks. Still, all of that would be moot if he dropped a bombshell after dropping me. By the look on his face, he was gearing up to say something major, features working, his jaw tensing and twitching.

"I could never, ever want anyone else. I don't love anyone the way I love you." His voice was raspy, desperate.

Knowing he feels that way about me is way more moist-making than anything else I've ever experienced. His hands reach for my shoulders, then stop.

"Just tell me."

"Tessa. And Leo. I-I trust them. They're good friends. Such good friends. They're the only ones I could ever…"

"You're freaking me out. Considering that you're a vampire and I'm okay with it? That's pretty record-breaking, Robbie."

His fists curl like he is desperately trying to talk and to hold it in, all at once. His voice won out, breaking and rolling urgently as he spilled his secret. "They smell amazing. Powerful. Sweet. Strong. Rich. They must taste—" fangs slid down with a wet shhh and his eyes were suddenly splashing waves of red into the blue oceans I love "—amazing."

"Oh, fuck," I gasped at the naked hunger in his eyes that swiftly directed itself toward me. He lunged onto the bed with me, nipping and kissing my pulse point, hands hurrying my faded green shirt over my head, hand tugging his black leather belt loose.

"Leo would let me. He knows what it's like to hunt without harming. Tessa… Tessa might not, that's okay. I would never, ever hurt them. I'd never touch a drop without your permission. It's just hard sometimes," he whimpered as he thrust up against my denim-clad crotch, making me moan and spasm inside. "Always knowing how good everyone smells, imagining how they would taste, and knowing you shouldn't drink. I don't want to become one of the evil ones, Charlotte. I want to be safe. I want to be safe with you. Safe with them."

I nod, unable to speak. Fangs slip in me and my eyes go dark with desire. My pussy floods at the sudden adrenaline rush and then floods with him. Robbie fills me completely without any of his usual foreplay.

I like it. The little bit of demon in me loves when he lets loose, because then I can, too.

Thoughts tangle in my head. Mainly thoughts about how he is growling as he sips on me, hands clutching wrists, legs up over his waist as we find a rhythm, finally settling on the fast pump of blood from my veins to his.

Confused? To ordinary humans, being bitten must be terrifying. For one thing, your brain is yelling "MONSTERS ARE REAL!" and "I'M GONNA DIE!" That's entirely possible if the vampire doing the biting cut ties to humanity and is living off victims. To a vampire who wants to live with humans, to a human who knows what's about to happen, who loves the rush... Oooh. I'd say they don't make words, but they do have one simple description that fits. Orgasmic.

I pant suddenly as his hips slam into mine and his fingers claw over my clit, rubbing in hard, fast circles as he pumps into me. "Robbie..."

"Fuck, Lottie, you taste so beautiful." He gulps and swallows, then licks my neck lingeringly, sending all nerves to battle stations. The blood ceases to flow and the scar heals over at once. Yay for demonic bloodlines and those weird cellular things that Tessa mentioned.

"H-how do you think..." I hesitate. I want to ask how Tessa would taste. Leo was somehow safer, though. "How do you think Leo tastes? How would you guys do this?"

He answers without blushing. That's good. It means he doesn't think there is anything shameful in whatever he has been imagining. I count cheating on the woman you want to marry shameful, so I rub his back encouragingly as his eyes simmer down and his fangs slip back into his upper jaw. He steadies his rhythm and rocks into me more slowly. In a second, he'll lay on me and I'll shift, taking the top, staring down at the amazing canvas of his pretty chest, all white flesh, and marble-carved muscles.

"He'll let me. Leo once told me that werewolves have packs. He doesn't. Not a pack of other werewolves, that is. He told me we're his pack and packs hunt together. They raise their pups together."

Well, now he blushes. Leo and Tessa will have kids. Not us. "It's okay," I whisper. "We'll help with their pups." I wink, trying not to imagine all the little ones that I'd never carry. If I want it bad enough, we'd work it out. Donors. Adoption. Surrogates. Something.

"You're right. You shouldn't have to give up all the—"

"Shut up, or I'll take the necklace off," I warn.

"I want to see you in that necklace and nothing else. Riding me. Watching it bounce," he breathes over my tingling skin. Robbie rolls off and waits for me to take charge.

I slide off the panties he'd torn to the side and he shucks off his jeans and socks. My sandals had long ago hit the floor. Bare except for my new pre-engagement gift, I mount his straining cock, stopping to bend down and slowly slip my lips around him. He growls in longing. I take my time coming off of him, his tongue finding salty-sweet traces of my first orgasm and long, cool drips of his pre-cum. "You taste beautiful, too." I wink.

"C'mere, Babes," he hisses insistently, gripping my shoulders and hurrying me away. "You'll undo me and I can't think straight."

"You can think straight watching this?" I demand, sliding on him and leaning forward to make my C-cups do their best work, pressed together in sumptuous hills as my hands rest on his chest, hard nipples inches from his pecs, the emerald jumping on each stroke.

"No," he admits.

I have demon blood. I mentioned that, right? I'm not evil. I'm not soulless. Demons have souls unless they sell, trade, or give them away. Many do. Human thoughts and rules are hard to play by when you have an unlimited lifespan and way more power than anyone else around you. A lot of demons get rid of that pesky soul so they can do what they want. I have a soul. But there's still that hint of demon. Maybe that's why sometimes, like right now, I can be just a tiny bit wicked.

I lean back and spread my thighs wide, showing him the straining pink tunnel that was swallowing his cock.

"Ohhh, fuck, where's m'phone?" he groans, accent thickening.

"On the floor with your clothes," I laugh. I reach down and rub my clit for his hungry eyes. My fingertips fumble back the hood and show him how dark pink it is, all flushed with blood. I swipe my tongue over my fingers and rub hard, letting him feel my inner muscles involuntarily milking, spasming. "Tell me about Leo."

"Now?"

"Mhmm. While you fuck me."

"It's not about sex. I swear."

"But it feels so good. The way you do it, it makes me feel like I'm gonna cum in seconds." I realize that is something we had to address. "It will give them feelings like that, won't it? Sexual feelings. With you?"

"Oh. Yeah, I guess... Well, it's off then. That's not okay."

I bounce in silence. Robbie's torso relaxes, his eyes close.

Unselfish guy. He would never hurt a soul. He'd especially never hurt me. So if it was even a question of conflicted emotions or tangled up feelings, he was just going to let it go. Never explore. That didn't feel right to me, either.

"Do they know that?"

"Not unless you told Tessa."

"I did. Not in detail, just that it feels the opposite of bad. It's wonderful. Especially during sex."

"I love Leo, but I'm very, very straight. If he got aroused from this, I—" Robbie pauses, a weird look on his face.

I have the same look. We both realize it with a little laugh. "Leo'd be totally fine. Blunt. 'Hey, man. I get hard from that. That's cool with you?'" I mimic his stoic speech.

"I'll tell him. I wouldn't reciprocate. I mean," he didn't blush with his pallor, but I could tell from his suddenly downcast eyes that he would've blushed if he could. "I might get certain feelings. But we— he and I—no. Tessa'd be there. You'd be there."

I shiver. That's right. We'd be there, with our lovers. "The neck?"

"His arm. I can't do the neck with him. It's too weird."

"Honey. You're a vampire. He's a werewolf. We're in Vegas. Weird is relative."

"Well, then," he turns the tables on me, suddenly driving up into me, making me fall forward and use him for support. "I want to bite him. Feel that rich, demon-heavy blood in my mouth. I smell him. He's like dark rum in a copper mug, that's what he is. And steak. He pounds like the drums. When we're on stage together, I can feel him. I can feel his pounding heart, his pulsing blood. God. Thick, rich, heavy, heady..."

"Ohhh, shit. No, Robbie, don't. Giving me bad thoughts," I gasp before I can stop myself.

"About what? Leo?" His eyes were suddenly empty of desire, full of worry.

"No. Not exactly." About watching him and Leo. That. Not even in a sexy way. I don't know what's wrong with me.

Oh, right. Vegas. Moral forcefield.

"I'm fine. Sorry. Tell me about Tess."

"Tessa is so strong. She's light and quick, fluid, and has so much magic in her. She'd be like every wonder drug in creation, topped with a strawberry. No, with a raspberry. Tart, light, quick, sharp. You'd be there. You could hold her hand or something. I dunno. Would she be scared? I couldn't do it if she was scared. Maybe if Leo held her and I had you wrapped around me, holding her other hand? God, sounds like we're a ruddy four-headed octopus, doesn't it?"

My tone changes. "Don't stop," I beg. The image (not the weird octopus image) of the four of us all cozy and connected makes me feel safe. Not jealous. Not scared. Safe. And way too horny.

"You're gonna burst me, Char," he warns as I get to my knees, round cheeks slipping up and down, landing on his legs with a hard smack each time.

I moan as his hand joins the action, a slap, then a knead. "You can ask. If it feels safe to you like it does to me. I trust them. If they say no, it won't ruin things."

It was true. And that was amazing. We could ask them for anything, do anything, and respect each other through it all. I think. I hope.

"But you want 'em to say yes. Want it as much as I do. Feel how wet you are. A bloody river in your pussy," he slid his hand round my cheeks and came up soaking wet. His fingers tantalize me, traveling to his mouth. He shows me his talented tongue, licking off every trace. They were back, in my mouth this time, gently finger-fucking my lips, caressing my tongue as I hungrily taste my own wetness. His fingers leave, and I moan at the loss.

I wail with new fullness. Robbie slips one finger into my backdoor as I ride him to climax.

I love Robbie, only Robbie, only Robbie.

But part of me briefly wondered how good two pieces of male anatomy would feel inside me at once.

I collapse on him, chest heaving as he spurts in me.

In the sudden quiet, I hear Tessa's long, wailing keen. A purely animalistic roar from Leo follows.

"Geez, it's the quiet ones," I tease, face aflame. They heard us having sex.

We heard them having sex.

I bit my lip.

Robbie strokes my hair.

He's my best friend.

I'm his best friend.

We tell each other everything, even if it takes a while.

"Does this make you think weird, not exactly clean thoughts?" I ask, just as he demands,

"My mind's gone off to strange places, how about yours?"

"I DON'T WANT US TO share," Robbie tells me softly in the shower. "Not our bodies. Not our hearts."

"I agree. I understand."

"But when you share blood, things get intimate. Pleasurable. Maybe we could... Lord, I dunno, Sweetheart." He scrubs my back and then leans his forehead to my hair, sighing.

"We could be close. Without overlapping?" I suggest the best term my hazy, naughty brain can think of.

"How close? What are you imagining it'd be like?"

I imagined. Leo's arm in Robbie's mouth, Tessa rubbing his chest as I nibbled Robbie's ear, loving the purring noise he makes as he drinks. Watching two erections strain against jeans.

Watching Leo suddenly push Tessa to the floor and shove her skirt over her hips as Robbie dragged me into his lap and unzipped, cock on display right before it sheathed in me.

Knowing they were watching.

Knowing we were watching them.

"I don't know," I answer truthfully. I honestly don't know how to describe the sights I see in my mind and why I want them to become real. "Close enough to share without invading."

"I feel close to them. Closest to you."

We kissed, hands wandering between our bodies, about to begin again.

"Good friends do weird things for each other sometimes. With each other sometimes," I whisper as Robbie's lip briefly flirts with my teeth.

"And whatever we do in Vegas?" His cock rubs urgently in my palm, then against the slickness of my swollen pussy. "Who we share it with?"

"Stays in Vegas," I gasp as he squeezes inside. Outside, I heard Tessa scream out a low, guttural noise of pleasure. Leo grunts loudly in satisfaction. It occurs to me afresh that the master bathroom, the one with the lavish tub and rainfall shower, was between the suite's two bedrooms. My pussy twitches again, and I look at Robbie. His tongue slowly trails over his half-parted lips.

They're right against us, making love while we're making love.

I imagine the walls were gone.

I put my finger to Robbie's lips, and he nods, understanding. We take each other silently, listening to the symphony our friends make, the symphony we might soon be joining.

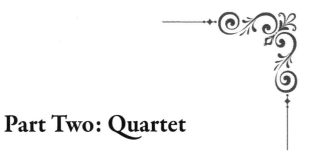

Part Two: Quartet

"D'you hear anything?" Robbie slowly sits up from the bed, where we ended up after our shower.

"*You* have the predator hearing," I remind him, putting my damp hair up in a loose bun. In reply, all I hear is a low, panther-like snarl. Oh. Right. Neck on display. It's like taking a thirsty vampire to a buffet. If the neck is attached to the naked body of his semi-fiancée, complete with swollen nipples and a puffy pussy that's freshly shaved, well...

I really have no one but myself to blame for the loving tackle and subsequent rugburn.

"LET'S TRY THIS AGAIN," Robbie pants and falls over, flopping onto his back.

"Well, you're still hard. I guess we could," I sigh, reaching for his slippery wet rod, slick with our juices.

"This is why I love you and wanna marry you," he moans and rolls on his side, white skin covered in scratches and semi-raw patches caused by the hotel's luxurious but stiff carpet. His head is on my breast, then my stomach, burying his face in the soft, semi-concave space, inhaling. "My demon queen."

Now, *that* one is a song by Skin Deep, the band Leo and Robbie front. Even though I'm no demon queen (I'm more like a demon thrice removed or something), I love the song.

Which Robbie is singing softly into my skin. "Demon queen, with your angel face, wicked eyes, and endless grace..."

"Do you guys want pizza?" Leo asks outside the door.

The song abruptly ends, and we both jump. I hear Tessa's muffled voice chiding, "I told you to wait until they came out!"

"Didn't know when that would be. Okay, guys. I'm getting the Meat Lover's Special!"

"Do you want me to get some extra juice from the bar downstairs? We can order it up?" Tessa calls worriedly.

"I'm fine! Yes about the pizza. So much yes!" I claw Robbie off of me, playfully fending off his grabby hands and his suckling kisses that leave nibble marks all over my chest and one hip. I know Tessa's juice comment is aimed at me. We made sure we found a butcher in the city limits before we made reservations, and Robbie's checked bag had a big block of dry ice with "juice pouches." However, human blood is more sustaining and lasts longer in a vampire's system. I think Tessa figured I would be his personal snack bar for a few days.

Hence, juice. See, that's a real friend. They understand if your boyfriend has special needs, and they don't judge. I want to go hug that girl, right now.

No, not right now. In a second. I need clothes. "Do I smell like sex?"

"Yes." Robbie is emphatic in this and his erection bobs in agreement as he stands.

"I need another shower." There is a tiny stall shower in our room. We didn't use it before because—well, shower sex. Duh.

"Okay. Sure." Robbie's voice was that bland, placating tone that he uses when he's agreeing to something he doesn't *actually* agree with.

"What?"

"Leo's nose. Uh." He rubs the back of his neck sheepishly. "And mine, for that matter. We always know, for hours afterward, even if you and Tessa shower a dozen times."

"Tessa, too?" I clapped my hand to my cheek. "Are you kidding me? You can tell when Tessa and Leo have— have been—"

"At it like it's their job? Yes. And he knows when you and I have been, too. Shower all you like if you feel dirty."

Feel dirty. Thinking about Robbie and Leo having such intimate knowledge of private activities, I found myself minding initially, and then...

Well, that shouldn't be sexy, should it?

It's not sexy. It's weird. I know it's weird.

"Does it turn you on?" I ask before my mouth and brain can finish sorting out what I *ought* to feel.

"No! Well... no. Not exactly. I don't find Tessa attractive. Not that she's ugly! She's very pretty"

I halt the Olympic-speed backpedal. "Calm down. I know she's cute and you don't find her attractive like that. Move on."

"I sort of find the idea of them together, mingling all those scents and flavors, all their powers together..." The red eyes were back.

"Vegas brings out everyone's weaknesses," I mumble. I march to the shower, only to find a strong arm suddenly thrust in my face, blocking my way.

"You like it. Don't bother to lie. Parts of you always speak the truth." His knee is riding up between my thighs, turning my hips to him, letting my soft, freshly filled pussy squirm on him. I'm wet, and not just because I love when he cums deep inside more than anywhere else. There's definitely arousal added to the mix.

"First, I never lie to you. I avoid, I change the subject, and I may occasionally cram two doughnuts in my mouth at once, but I don't lie," I remind him. His contrite expression and majorly cute pout soften my tone. "The smelling thing is *not* sexy. Not to me, but then again, I don't have the same kind of triggers and senses. It's the idea of Leo and Tessa doing *things*. And them knowing we're doing things. Holy crap, Robbie, I'm turning into a voyeur."

"Do you want to go watch Mr. and Mrs. Jones down the hall get it on?"

"Eww! No!"

"Then you're not a voyeur. You're just considerin' things because we're all cozy this weekend. 'Cause sex is runnin' riot. Because I told you I want a taste and you know when I get a taste it only wakes up other appetites." His London drawl was thicker, hands creeping up my waist, fingers ending on my ribcage, palms squeezing my breasts.

"Oh, fuck, Robbie!" I put my feet down and drag him with me into the tiny cubicle.

"There's no bloody room in this—"

"Shut up and make it fast. Pizza's coming." I scale him like he's my private ladder, knees over his hips, elbows over his shoulders to hoist myself up, and then take the plunge down, our bodies jammed into space barely big enough for one. He's buried inside of me, the two of us becoming one. After the initial bout of moaning and gasping, I urge him to top speed with hard clenches of my tight pink walls.

"Gonna burst me in seconds," he protests.

"It's cramped and I'm hungry," I whisper. We snicker together before the moaning resumes.

I KNOW, I KNOW. I DON'T sound very romantic sometimes. If you're madly in love with your best friend, sometimes you don't do hearts and flowers. (I vaguely recall sex in my dorm room being punctuated by a Stanley Cup match and a hunt for nose spray. Even one-quarter demon chicks get sick once in a while.)

To be honest, watching Robbie almost die of cancer wasn't very romantic. All his beautiful hair fell out. He looked more dead than he does now. He threw up on me once. He threw up often. He needed so many blood transfusions. And later, we shared macabre chuckles about how him trading up to vampire status was just another kind of transfusion. (Yes, we know. We're effed up people.)

Sometimes we're light on the romance. We're always heavy on the love.

I don't love anyone more than my parents and Robbie. Tessa and Leo are a very close second.

"THIS IS THE BEST WEEKEND ever!" I emerge from our room at top speed, suddenly unable to control these mushy feelings, at least now that I'm dressed.

Tessa squeals and screeches into me, throwing herself into my arms. We jump up and down and giggle like idiots. "We're in Vegas!"

"I just turned twenty-one!"

"I'm turning twenty-one in three days!"

"Champagne!" I declare.

"Two bottles!" Tessa agrees.

"I'm so glad you're here!"

"I'm so glad you're here!"

"I love you!"

"I love you!"

"This is why we're besties!" More giggling.

"Beer?" Leo's voice is mildly amused.

"Please." Robbie takes a can.

"They're oddly similar. But I dig it." The placid werewolf toasts Robbie, cans clinking.

"To good women. The best women."

"To our women. That's not a sexist, possessive thing, by the way. More like when you talk about your life partner. I'm perfectly willing to be called your man," Leo informs Tessa, a smirk on his thin lips.

"You can possess me all you want," Tessa giggles, releasing me in favor of snuggling up to Leo.

The display of affection is nice and a little bit shocking. Before this weekend, I think I've seen them kiss a handful of times over several years. Tessa is super shy, and Leo is quiet, more likely to answer with nods ninety percent of the time, and then come out with something insanely witty or philosophical the other ten percent. They hold hands frequently, stare at each other, and smile like they're having whole conversations telepathically.

I find myself staring as their kiss doesn't stop.

"Hungry, Babes?" Robbie's voice is low and close to my ear, double-edged in his meaning. Am I hungry watching our best friends or hungry because the pizza smells divine, and I must've burned a few thousand calories since we arrived?

"Both," I answer.

He nods at me with a grave face, knowing exactly what I mean. Guess Tessa and Leo aren't the only ones who do the telepathic thing.

"Let's eat."

"WHY DIDN'T WE ORDER four?" Tessa throws the second empty box off the coffee table.

"Because I grossly underestimated how much you two would eat," Leo answers, picking up the hotel phone again.

"Hey!" Tessa and I let out twin cries of indignation.

"No one's complaining. Everyone needs to refuel. Can you think of any nobler cause than Vegas vacation sex?" Robbie groans and leans back.

I dart him a look. Okay. So, the S-word is out there now. The four of us have been pawing and kissing all night, Leo and Tessa, Robbie and me. We've made hints about how great the rooms are, how nice the beds are, and how much fun this vacation has already been without even leaving the room. All those hints have been dropped. Robbie and Leo have been moving slowly toward the center of the huge L-shaped couch until they are knee-by-knee.

It is quite the picture. Robbie has dark hair and marble skin, carved lips, and high cheekbones. Classically handsome, my mother proclaimed, just about swooning the first time she met him. Leo is rugged and square-jawed, with shoulders that are several inches broader than Robbie's, but also lower down on his shorter frame. His skin is naturally pale, not as pale as Robbie's, but he also seems to prefer indoor spaces and nights lately. Top all that off with gloriously thick auburn hair that's starting to fall over hazel eyes. Eyes that are—hungry. Predatory.

"You want more?" Leo asks in a voice that is closer to a growl than human speech.

I'm lost. More what? He's asking Robbie. More pizza? Another beer? Are they talking about sex? More out of life, in the grand scheme of things?

I look at Tessa in admiration. How she can live with a guy who has such an economy of words is beyond me.

"Yeah..." Robbie turns to him, head almost brushing his. Something is passing between them, silent and electrical, unseen and unspoken, but obviously there.

I find my hand suddenly on Tessa's arm. Something's going to happen in the next few minutes. I need to touch her, make sure she won't vanish. Whatever happens, all of it has to be okay. Whatever happens next, when Robbie tells him about wanting a very specific, intimate type of drink, and whatever response Leo and Tessa have... we have to stay together. We can't lose them.

Tessa winds her slender, petite fingers through mine. "Is everything—"

"I... I get hungry. I'm not hungry, literally. Not starving. I have blood. I'm fine. This isn't survival. I want to—I want to taste someone. Be close to them. Taste their power. Someone I trust." Robbie turns his head away, back to me. I'm instantly walking toward him. That must've been so hard to say. So hard to risk telling his best friend, his almost-brother, his bandmate. Robbie is brave in all kinds of ways. I love him for each and every one.

"Oh." Leo doesn't look ruffled. If he gets how hard that was for Robbie, he's not making it a big deal. "I'm guessing that's not something you can ask most people. Your uncle? Charlotte, of course."

"Bertie isn't an option." Robbie swallows hard. Leo's eyes shift, then his whole head turns.

"You good?"

"Yeah. I'm fine, I—" He moves to rise, but Leo tilts his head and rivets him, nostrils wide.

"Fear? You're not even afraid of me when I wolf out. You barely blink." Leo suddenly turns his head to lock eyes with Tessa and me. "Is this a guy thing?"

"No, they have to stay!" Robbie blurts, voice strangled.

"Oh! Oh, not Bertie because of the *feelings*!" Tessa's voice is a soft gasp, eyes wide.

Big brain girl. She gets it.

"Feelings?" Leo raises one eyebrow. The gesture lengthens his face somehow and suddenly I see the wolf under the man, the elongated jaw that must form, the eyes that must dilate to hunt in the dark.

"Feelings," Tessa repeats significantly, her hips unconsciously swaying with a little thrust in her lover's direction.

I have to clarify before everything goes south.

I picture Leo's head going south, down between Tessa's open legs, and I—

Oh my God. I don't even watch dirty movies! I mean, Robbie and I will occasionally consult a helpful website for a new position or something, but, this is like…

Damn.

Back to clarifying. "Robbie's only ever bitten me. I've only ever been bitten by him. It feels wonderful. Not painful. Decidedly sexual. The act itself isn't sexual, but, um… when we do it, it seems that way."

"By default. She's my girl. I'm her guy," Robbie explains, reaching shakily for the last unopened can in the six-pack. "Want to taste a new flavor of blood, with someone I can trust, who trusts me. If we—if there were feelings, you'd know I wasn't having them for you. This is not coming out right. I need another drink."

"No, you don't." Leo shakes his head. He rises, and moves to Tessa, who drifts to him like oceans are tethered to the moon. His arm goes possessively around her waist. "Char?"

"Here," I croak, quickly sliding next to Robbie on the couch, my arm around his slouching shoulders. He looks confused and angry with himself. The physical distance that just happened, and the sudden shift that looks like couple facing down couple has me momentarily worried, too.

But there's nothing hostile in Leo's voice or Tessa's soft expression. They analyze. They overthink. They don't freak (usually). "Robbie does the biting. He enjoys it. I'm not worried about that. I mean, when I sink my fangs into a nice fresh buck during a full moon..." He licks his lips. For a second, I swear I see his incisors ridging down, wolf-like teeth sprouting among his reminiscent smile. "I get enjoying your meal."

"Not a meal!" Robbie thumps his fist on his knee. "I made a right mess of this. Forget it. Can you forget it, please?"

"If you want me to. I was planning to ask a couple of questions and then take my shirt off. I like this shirt." He pokes the thin cotton shirt he's wearing. "No blood on it. I don't know if you're a messy eater."

I flash an extremely grateful grin at my best male best friend outside of Robbie. Robbie's head jerks back, hope in his eyes, not because he might get a drink, but because Leo doesn't want to run from him.

"If you get good feelings, okay. But will I? Char? As resident vampire bite-ee, you have the floor."

"I do. I was thinking you might. I don't know. Maybe it's only because Robbie and I are involved. If you did, though, Tessa and you could... slip away." Or not. Stay right here. Next to us.

Tessa's pale skin turns hibiscus pink. "And you and Robbie would... take care of things, too?"

"Right."

"Just me?" Leo asks.

Wait. What? Is he asking what I think he's asking?

Robbie's eyes dart between the three of us, and linger on Tessa a shade too long, a tad too apologetically. He got cold feet in the middle of talking to Leo about it and now he doesn't want to complicate it more by asking Tessa.

Tessa is an angel of mercy. She has the softest heart of anyone I've ever met. She rescues wasps caught in windows and cries at Hallmark commercials, including the funny ones with Snoopy. Robbie is another wounded bird to rescue at the moment. "Oh. Oh! Me? That's fine. If it's fine with everyone else." Her voice quivers and her eyes are blinking too fast in surprise. But her smile is comforting.

I think Robbie is about to cry in relief or joy, which would be sweet, but just make everything a million times more awkward. (If there is a world record for Most Awkward Conversation, we're already in the running.) I quickly speak up, "We can all be together and it's very safe. He doesn't need much to stay full. Human blood is more filling for vampires than animal blood. Blood from part-humans, humans with powers, is even better. He won't need much from us because we're already powerful."

"I only want a little taste. I can smell how good you taste," Robbie finishes lamely. His confidence is coming back as Tessa and Leo join us on the couch, boys back together in the middle.

Leo nods and moves to pull his shirt over his head, but Robbie stops him. "The arm. Doesn't need to be in your neck."

"Promise not to spill?" Leo gives Robbie a half-smirk.

"I'll buy you a bottle of bleach, okay?"

"You'll be buying me a new shirt, dude."

"Deal. I owe you one."

"Hey. You take me out to run wild when no one else can. I figure I owe you a few dozen at least." Leo's arm is out, stiff and straight like he's about to give blood at the doctor.

I don't know if I want it to be that quick and clinical.

I know that I want it to be anything but. I wrap my arm around Robbie's waist, scrunched in behind him, my leg in terry lounging shorts draped over his jean-covered knee. Tessa leans herself to Leo's back, pretty lip pulled in between her teeth, her sundress straps slipping as she leans with him, showing small hills of cleavage.

I think Tessa must be soft all over, as soft as Robbie is hard.

My hand comes to rest on Robbie's chest as his face transforms slowly. It's odd how I still expect to feel his heart thudding. Mine is racing.

"Thanks, Brother." Robbie takes the arm and pulls firmly, head bowing.

"Any time." Leo moves closer, his eyes watching without wariness. More like curiosity. I see him reach back and twine his fingers with Tessa's.

I mentioned that Pine Ridge is suburbia with a twist, right? People like us, people with something extra, have seen a vampire before, but not usually with their fangs out. I think Robbie and Leo are used to seeing each other like this because of their "hunting trips."

Tessa may have seen Robbie in fangs a couple of times.

But not like this.

This time her breath catches audibly, and Robbie's scarlet irises dart to hers as his fangs hover a millimeter above Leo's hard, pale forearm. She doesn't move. Doesn't tell him no. Doesn't smile. Or frown. Tessa's frozen, waiting in limbo.

I mouth something. I think I say, "It's okay." Honestly, Tessa might be frozen, but she trusts Robbie and whatever he's doing. If Tessa doesn't like something, she can obliterate it with a well-placed stare.

That's our girl.

"Just go," Leo says calmly. If he is creeped out or uncomfortable, it doesn't show. I don't think he feels any such thing. If I need more proof, he gives it to me. "What, do I suddenly not smell good?" His head tilts back toward Tessa, and his hand moves from her hand to her thigh, squeezing it. She gasps, lips parting, knees twitching open. "Do you think I'm going to taste like something else?"

Do you know how secret agent guys have "wake words?" Those secret code words that zap them into attack mode?

I don't know exactly what Leo said (I think it was the things he didn't say, things he only hinted at), but Leo has Robbie's wake word.

A hiss, a smile, and a harsh little whisper send rivers running through me, all heading south. "You taste like the hunt. Adrenaline, all bottled up. Just waiting to let it fly," Robbie tells Leo as they lock eyes. In less than a heartbeat, fangs slice in and dig deep.

There's a quiet cacophony. Leo and Robbie make their own sort of primal, pleasurable noises. Tessa and I gasp from the spectator seats, which become instantly less spectator-y.

Robbie has a death grip on Leo's arm with one hand, and his other reaches back to snag me in a grip that screams "mine." It's a song of possessiveness, sex, and heat, all in five fingertips.

Leo's hand digs into the patterned pink fabric between Tessa's thighs, dragging it up as he pulls her closer, his bruising grip turning into insistent kneading. Any second, I imagine his growl will turn into a contented purr as his jaw goes slack and his eyes turn into black pools of pleasure.

"Fuck..." Leo breathes out.

"That's next," I say, not thinking clearly. Leo's reclining. His dark cotton pajama pants are pulled taut in the front. Tessa licks her lips, gasp turning into a moan.

"Is it that good?" she asks, rubbing Leo's shoulders.

I nod, trying not to say something crude. "There's your evidence." That's all I can manage as Leo arches his spine, his hips thrusting forward.

Robbie lifts his mouth, gulping hastily, not a drop spilled on the precious shirt. His eyes are wide and joyful. "Oh my God. That's amazing. Thank you. Thank you," he laughs, almost giddy. He lunges forward to hug Leo, who thumps him on the back. "Thanks, Babe." He turns and scoops me up, hugging me tightly.

I know what he's thanking me for. For letting him try this, for not turning it into something huge.

He leans across Leo and grasps Tessa's hand, squeezing it enthusiastically, little tremors of relief and joy coursing down his shoulders. "Thanks, Tessa. Thank you, sweetie, you're an angel."

"I thought I was the angel," I tease, not jealous at all. I just don't know how to handle this tension. It's decidedly sexual, and my heart screams *Robbie*, and my hips scream *Robbie*, and my brain and eyes whisper that if we all stay together, we'll get a new kind of treat.

"Nnn-nnn," he inhales against my neck, hands cradling my hips, pulling me tight to his erection. "You're my demon queen. Mmm, my love, my life, my future bride." Each sweet word earns a nip against my pulse points, making me spasm back, showing off the extra suppleness in my spine.

Robbie whirls me back up, half over his shoulder, still laughing. "Are you okay?"

He's not talking to me, though. I guess we got so caught up in being happy that Leo didn't freak out before or during, that we forgot to check on the after.

Leo is still reclining, the hungry look in his eyes magnified. He hasn't spoken since Robbie broke contact. "That's intense. And kinda weird."

"Well, we're demons in Vegas for a long weekend, so..." Robbie laughs, but I know there's a little anxiety under the humor.

"I never got turned on by a guy before."

"Well, technically you didn't get turned on by Robbie. Did you?" Tessa squeaks.

Leo's head nearly breaks off his spine from the speed of his turn. "You're the only thing I want. Ever." He kisses Tessa with his hands clutching her so hard that his already pale skin blanches white.

"Bad choice of words," I soothe when they come up for air, panting, heads still dancing together, little lip brushes, fingers stroking through auburn bangs and long red tresses.

"Totally. Never... I never got hard from something I experienced with another guy around. Or caused by the other guy. It's kinda... head trippy. I like it though. I'd give it a ten on the things to do in Vegas. Bonus—" Leo examines his arm, which has already stopped bleeding from the tight, neat little holes Robbie gave him, "there was no cover charge and it's portable. Frankly, it's way better than weed. Cheaper. Helps a buddy out. The side effects are awesome."

Robbie snorts, shifting around on the couch with an amused, lopsided grin. "That's right, folks. Tune in later for Professor Leo's discussion on relaxation. Today's topic, the benefits of vampire bites versus CBD oil."

Tessa snickers as well. "Help the hungry. Get horny."

"Tess!" I squeal, laughing, too. That's like a level ten on the raciness scale for my typically quiet bestie.

Being slightly tipsy and "shagged out" (as Robbie would say) continues to loosen Leo's tongue. "I'd say we could do it when the band goes on tour in July, but not unless the girls come with us."

"Mhm. Immediate girlfriend loving required." The nips turn into snuffles, the kisses on my shoulders work with his massaging hands. Robbie pulls the loose cotton down to expose the skin where his mouth latches on.

"No complaints here," I sigh. He has a talented mouth. Talented hands. His hips jerked pointedly up, my damp shorts indenting from the hardness he's shifting me to straddle. Talented cock. The things this man can do... Even before he joined the immortal club, Robbie had all the moves.

Now he just keeps them going for a few hours at a time.

"Maybe we'd better get out of here?" Tessa asks breathlessly, her eyes speaking volumes as they merge with Leo's lustful gaze.

At this point, Robbie and I probably wouldn't mind if several elephants entered or exited our suite, as long as they gave us about two feet of space on the couch. (Or the floor, against a wall, a coffee table... you get the idea.) If Leo and Tessa want to go take care of the obvious trouser equipment Leo's sporting, they have my blessing. In fact, they have my vocal encouragement. I want them to leave immediately, so I can pull my sopping shorts to the side, unzip Robbie, and plunge myself down on him. I want him inside until he bottoms out in me, balls deep, tip up against my g-spot, so full it almost hurts and— Fuck, why are my loyal best friends being so particularly loyal at this damn moment? "Sure. Go," I moan. Robbie's nudges put me on the verge of needing to touch myself if he doesn't.

"No, wait." Leo's voice puts a dent in my fantasy. "Tessa didn't get a turn."

Never mind. New fantasy.

"But, Robbie's all... y'know." Her cheeks abandon hibiscus and head for pomegranate.

"And so am I." Leo, ever surprising, has a perfectly logical solution for staying. "It's incredible. Very... heightening. I didn't want you to feel left out. I got to experience it, you should, too. If Robbie still wants to."

Robbie and I steal a split-second glance. This is seriously the most awkward blend of inappropriateness and etiquette ever invented.

Only in Vegas. Is it more polite to excuse ourselves to have loud, screaming, XXX-rated sex in private, or more polite to increase our friend's chances of having the same sort of action through decidedly questionable methods?

"It's up to Tess." Robbie slips me from his lap.

Mistake. Now Tessa and I have an eyeful of two *very* erect male specimens, specimens that we love and adore, specimens that are fuckably hot even fully clothed and not panting at us with lustful eyes and spitting sensuality like sexy cobras.

"I—uh, I... C'mere!" Tessa dives for me and grabs me by the wrist, tripping over a pizza box as we suddenly barrel into the huge master bathroom.

"You don't have to! I mean, it doesn't hurt, but it's still not for everyone," I say as soon as she slams the door.

"He's hard!"

"I know."

"Well. Uh." My articulate friend has gone tongue-tied. "I mean. Can I—can he bite me if he's hard?"

"Never stops him from biting me." I shrug.

"Char! That's not what I mean and you know it. There are some seriously sexual vibes right now."

"Yeah, but Robbie doesn't want to have sex with you. Leo wants to have sex with you. He wants you to enjoy it as much as he will, and he got a boost from Robbie."

"What about you?"

"Oh, he already bit me. He'll bite me again later. Don't worry. He's not going to get a stomachache or anything."

I think Tessa wants to slap me. But instead, she hugs me, sighing and shaking her head. "It looked exciting."

"To put it mildly."

"You don't mind?"

"No! Look, you love chocolate cake, right?"

"Enough to consider getting it tattooed on my ankle. If I was a tattoo-having sort of person."

"Do you remember freshman year of college? When you found out that they ALWAYS served chocolate cake in the dining hall?"

There's a wince. I share it. I've never seen someone throw up so much brown stuff before.

"That was a rookie mistake. I learned to pace myself."

"The point being, Robbie loves me. I'm his chocolate cake. And you're—" I try to recall exactly what he said about the woman next to me, and then I spin it a little. "You're like raspberry mousse, light, quick, and sharp. Powerful, beautiful, and soft. He'd eat cake every day for the rest of his life, but a little piece of fruit every now and again adds some balance. And enjoyment."

"A lot of enjoyment," Tessa whispers, biting her bottom lip.

"Go get 'em, Tiger," I encourage, pushing her toward the door.

"Shouldn't that be go get gotten? Or something?"

"Just open the door!"

"I'm not a tiger!"

"Robbie's the tiger." I wink. "I know you like wolves, but visit another cage at the zoo."

"And he goes to another plate on the dessert cart?"

As an English major, I hate when people mix metaphors. But this fits, and I'm on vacation. "Exactly."

LEO SETTLES TESSA IN his lap, hands around her waist, knee between her thighs, pushing her forward, ostensibly so Robbie can have better access to her arm or neck, wherever they decide. However, by the sudden gasp she lets out, and the way her legs suddenly twitch, I know that Leo is like me. He lets the demon out to play a little bit, a touch of wickedness is used in fun. He likes to make her squirm the way Robbie and I make each other squirm. His hard knee is pressed up against her mound, his hard cock nestling between her cheeks.

I wonder if they ever—

I need bleach for my brain.

Later. On Tuesday. After this vacation is done.

It's weird watching Robbie touch Tessa's face so tenderly.

No, no, not like that. He's one of the most compassionate people I've ever met. He watched his mother die from cancer they couldn't beat, one that almost got him, too. He held her hand. Sang her to her final rest. I know that experience softened his heart, not hardened it, as it would many people. He's been with me through every bug I've contracted, every not-so-nice demon who doesn't belong in Pine Ridge, every bad thing since he met me.

Robbie has a drop-dead gorgeous heart. He'd never hurt a soul.

I blink suddenly. Stupid tears trying to infiltrate what ought to be a purely fun, sexy occasion. It's not fair that such a good guy gets lumped in with all the evil ones because he has new dental appendages.

"I promise it doesn't hurt more than a pinprick, not if you relax. If you want to. You know I love you, Tess. You bein' my friend, bein' Charlotte's best friend, that's enough of a gift," he whispers, low and slow, the English accent more pronounced when he's emotional.

The accent alone is enough for most girls to agree to anything. Plus, that face. And that body.

> Holy shit, I'm so horny right now.
> "I'm not worried," Tessa murmurs.

"Really? You wouldn't lie to me?" He gives her a smile that's playful around the edges and serious in the middle. It's a Robbie smile. It matches him.

It occurs to me that I have seen him do this before. The time Tessa fell down a flight of stairs on Move-Out Day at the dorm. She broke her ankle, and he kept her calm while I ran back to our room, found the book she needed, and she did a spell to fix the fracture.

"You always take good care of us." Tessa smiles with glimmering eyes. She remembers, too.

Just as things are about to get soppy, Leo nudges her hard with his knee and she winces in pleasure, petite curves on display, neck arching back.

Robbie's eyes head to the red zone and his teeth accompany them.

"Arm," Leo says firmly as Robbie's head moves toward hers.

"Arm," Robbie agrees, head now dipping. He connects with a light, chaste kiss, like some old-time gentleman pecking a lady's wrist as they head off to the opera.

I know I should be watching Tessa. This is the newest and scariest to her at this point. But as Robbie's fangs slowly slip into her and rubies pile up on the edge of his smile, my eyes find Leo's.

He's watching them, too, splitting attention in that calm, almost clinical way that he has. His hand slowly moves to take a hold of Tessa's breast.

He massages her while he's looking at me, and it's not a dirty look. It's a... a question.

My hand moves into Robbie's lap as I lean my cheek to his shoulder.

The tiniest nod passes from his chin to mine.

Robbie said Leo knew.

Leo knows a whole fucking lot and he's nice about it.

He's part wolf. Wolves don't have as many inhibitions.

Add that to Vegas and...

"Isn't that amazing, baby?"

"Oh. Oh, ohhhhh. Oh, my God!" Tessa is quivering and her hand suddenly rakes through Robbie's dark brown hair, fingers anchoring down and tugging. But she's not pulling him off, she's pushing him in deeper.

"I love this. I love this, oh my God, this is .... Oh my God." Her hips flutter and bounce.

Leo's grin widens. Squirming accomplished. "You can go with it," Leo whispers.

Robbie sits up with one final pull. It wasn't more than two minutes. "Light and airy. Sponge cake and mint. Raspberry." He licks her arm slowly, punctures sealing up as he dances over her skin.

"Th-that was really good," Tessa stammers, neck blotchy and face flushed with rushing, arousal-fueled blood.

"I owe you. Thank you, sweetie." Robbie moves toward her with a grateful hug.

Tessa is sandwiched, Robbie hugging her, Leo holding her.

I am so envious it's not even funny.

"This was a group thing. Get in here." Tessa makes sure I'm included in the group hug.

The group hug. "Group thing." There are too many hard parts and soft parts, and we're all jostling and nuzzling. It's beautiful and loving and all that—but if I don't get something hard pumping in and out of me in the next thirty seconds, I might explode.

That'll be hell on the room deposit.

Robbie squishes me in. There's bumping and grinding, rough denim and brass on the skin of my bare stomach. My shirt is somehow hitched up.

There's a hand under it. It's Robbie's. I can tell because it's cooler than normal human skin, but not by much. But right next to me, literally against me, I feel Leo's hand through two layers of fabric. We're turning, trying to make sure everyone is part of this not-exactly-mushy tangle. I feel knuckles on my left breast as Leo's hand does something to Tessa's right, something that makes her moan and lean forward so that her cheeks are pressed into his groin- which just means she's way too close to me.

"Wh—" Robbie can't ask what's happening, but I know he wants to. We talked about this, but it was all talk.

"Wanna see our room?" I blurt.

Oh, my effing brain.

"Lottie!" Robbie hisses.

"Yeah," Tessa breathes, lips so close I can feel her words, not just hear them.

"It's all good, right?" Leo looks at Robbie, who nods immediately. "I love her."

He means Tessa. It's a very simple statement with a very simple meaning. I love Tessa. She is mine. You touch my lover and I'll rip your pretty throat out.

"I love her." Robbie's head jerks hard toward me, landing cheek to cheek, so we stare at them, eye to eye, so close our foreheads almost touch.

"So, it's all good."

What the hell that means, I have no idea. I guess we're going to go find out.

THE POSH SUITES ON the Las Vegas strip are meant for freakiness. You can tell by the beds. I mean that honestly. You can tell just by the sheer proportions of the furnishings. This bed could sleep six, and I imagine it has. It has plenty of room for four people and a no-man's land in between.

Am I thinking about having sex in the same bed as my best friends, while they're in it also having sex? Yes, yes, I am. That shouldn't sound so icky yet awesome.

"Wh-what are we doing?" Tessa falls onto her adorable rump on the right side as I crawl up onto the left. Leo stands beside her, and Robbie sits on the edge next to me.

"Keeping the good feelings going," Leo answers as if it's obvious. "Shared sexual energy."

"Shared as in nearby. Not swapping. I don't want this to be confusing. Or weird," I pipe up.

"Too late for weird, babes," Robbie sighs.

"You think too much." Leo strips his shirt off as my jaw plummets.

"This comin' from the biggest brain on campus, barring Tessa's," Robbie scoffs, his own shirt tossed off, belt snaking out after it.

The way he does that, both hands at his crotch to undo the belt buckle, rounding his shoulders, but looking up... sweet Jesus. Every inch of muscle is taut and perfect, pulling the neck muscles tight, showing the ridges and hills of his abs. I've seen it on a daily basis, but it doesn't get any less hot. I would very gladly climb aboard in front of fifteen thousand with stadium seating. Two quiet bystanders? No big deal.

"Lights!" Tessa yelps and snaps her fingers. The lights go dark with an acrid tang in the air. "Oops."

"We have these inventions called light switches, Witchie-Poo," I tease, voice slightly hoarse.

"There was about to be guy parts on display!" Tessa hisses. Clearly, Tessa deems those kinds of emergencies worthy of witchcraft-—and frying the bedroom fuses.

"Just guy parts? Where's the fun in that?" Robbie's voice is liquid silk, sliding down my back as his hands slip up my front. I shiver, topless in seconds, and suddenly remember that Leo can see in the dark. I swallow. Robbie can, too. If they want to. It's a simple matter of keeping human irises at the forefront.

"I'm not peeking if you aren't," Leo informs us.

Well, damn it, I want to see. The action, not the bodies, necessarily. I've caught glimpses of Tessa over the years. We were college roommates before we split off into coupledom. I've seen Leo at the pool—top half only. The dude is ripped in a completely different way than Robbie. Robbie looks like a piece of sculpture. Leo looks like an athlete, muscular, but lean. Maybe it's because of his square jaw and the fact that he's a little shorter when he's next to Robbie that it makes him seem broader. Everything about Leo speaks in planes and solid mass whereas Robbie is all angles and lines.

"That's fine," Tessa says. Is it just my fevered imagination, or does she sound the tiniest bit disappointed? Too bad if she is. She fried the wiring.

I forget about that though. Thirty seconds have passed, and Robbie is now completely, gloriously nude next to me on the bed, our hands are hurrying together to get my shorts off. Beside me, I hear the rustle of fabric and soft, passionate little moans. Tessa and Leo aren't the talking type, I guess. All about the kissing.

Well, my mouth is busy just now anyway.

"Oh, fuck, I love you, Char." Robbie is NOT the silent type. As my mouth slips up and down his length, I can't help but revel in his breathless groans. He's not even going to try to hide how good I make him feel.

"Oh, oh, ohhh. Ohh!" Soft moans that abruptly crescendo. A yelp and yip and something very wet sounding is happening next to me.

Leo's lapping Tessa's pussy. With great expertise, apparently.

"That sounds like a good idea," Robbie's voice is a husky chuckle and I find my treat removed.

"Give that back!" I protest like a petulant child. "My Rob-sicle!"

"You'll get it back in two seconds. Give me your ankle."

A low chuckle beside us-—now in the vicinity of my head, about three feet away. "Rob-sicle," Leo laughs.

"Shut up, Fido," Robbie hisses, before his mouth descends on my hot and bothered pussy lips and his tongue dances its way inside.

I DON'T EVEN MEAN FOR it to happen. Imagine the god of all sexual pleasure (ie. Mr. Robbie Scarsdale, late of London and current resident of Pine Ridge, NY) is tongue-fucking your pussy and sucking on your clit and he decides to flip you over so he can slip two fingers in and out, too. You would flail around, right?

I flail. I smack Leo on the back. Not hard!

It's a very nice back. Broad and surprisingly smooth for a guy who looks like shag carpeting three days of every month. And he's still making my best friend sound extremely happy. Moaning and whimpering, and cursing very creatively, in both Latin and English.

Show off.

So, my hand lingers a second. I pat. Like, job well done. And then it rests on Tessa's smooth, silky calf for a second. A second, I swear.

Tessa jumps a mile and Leo growls. I thought he was angry, but it turns out he just was ready to move to the next stage of things. He slides up her body and pulls her halfway down the bed to meet him.

It is perfectly innocent.

As innocent as four not-quite normal people in one bed fucking each other's brains out can be innocent, that is.

YOUR EYES ADJUST IN the dark. Even human eyes. Leo is on his knees, Tessa's knees up under his arms, her delicately arched feet crossed on the small of his back as he slams into her. Frankly, I have no idea how such a tiny little body accommodates that much pounding. I'll ask her later.

When I'm not getting pounded so hard myself.

We end up in opposite directions, by which I mean my head is somewhere near the middle-foot region of the bed, and Tessa's head is near the top.

"Oh, wow. Wow," she breathes out, but her cries were different.

Her head isn't looking up toward her lover's face.

It isn't staring at Robbie.

It is pointed where Robbie and I are moving together.

"Wow?" I gasp, an edge of laughter in my voice.

"Um. I—Oh."

I experiment, feeling very bold, and nervous as heck. I take my knee up to my chest. If my leg was obscuring the sight of Robbie's long white cock slipping in and out of my leaking pussy, it wasn't anymore.

"Oh, shit. Shit, Lottie. Lottie's so pretty. You and Robbie are the most beautiful thing I've ever— but not more beautiful than you!" Her babble of praise and awe that is directed at us shifts guiltily at Leo. We all laugh, except for Tessa, who pouts. I flap my hand around until I find her fingers and squeeze the reassuringly.

"We should return the favor," Leo announces and unhooks her legs while she squeaks. She moans. Even in the dark, I can feel her blushing. But she doesn't stop him. In fact, she turns slightly toward me.

Tessa's pussy is bare except for a fine strip of glossy reddish hair. Her inner lips are tight and heart-shaped, with her clit a prominent pearl on top. Leo, without any sense of shyness at all, pulls his thick, wet cock completely out of her slit and shows me her pouting pink pussy, its tunnel slightly gaping from the battering it had taken.

I couldn't speak. All the air leaves my lungs. My throat closes up.

Is this what anaphylaxis feels like? No. That's always reported as utterly terrifying. This is... so bad, on so many levels, but the pleasure zinging through me isn't scary enough to make me stop.

I want to touch her. Feel how wet she is. Slip my finger in and see if she moans for me, too. My hand is wandering that way.

Leo's fist is hard, and his eyes are bright, almost glowing as he smacks all five fingers down in an iron grip on my wrist. "No."

"Oi!" Robbie's eyes are suddenly red headlights in the black room.

There's a snarl, a growl, and the two men I love most in the world suddenly push the women they love most aside, grappling, hands smacking into chests, pushing off shoulders, the whole thing a scene out of some ancient book of primal drawings.

"Look. Not touch!" Leo growls low in his chest.

"Touch my bride again and I'll take your hand off," Robbie warns with equal menace.

"I'm sorry!" I wail. "I'm sorry! It was—she's so beautiful. I swear I wasn't thinking. Leo, Robbie, please don't—"

"Down." Tessa's voice is steel as she scrambles up, pillow clasped to her heaving torso. Leo stops snarling and sits, panting, confused looking. "Did I—"

"You almost savaged your best friend because my friend— Well, I'm not sure exactly what happened."

I feel confused and sick to my stomach at what I almost did. I'm not into girls, I'm into Robbie. But how often do you get to experiment in a safe place, especially with someone you love supporting you, and the other person you love being right there, all pouting and pink and pretty?

"Did I—did I wolf-out?" Leo blinks and rubs his eyes, breathing uneven.

"No. Almost."

"We can't play this kind of game." Robbie pulls me behind him and knots a towel cast off from our earlier shower around his waist. "She didn't do anything wrong. You showed her. You showed her..." His explanation dries up with a blush. We showed them, too. It was a sexy game of show and tell, of look, not touch, and I'm the one who broke the rules.

"I'm sorry. God, I'm sorry, too." Leo sits on the edge of the bed, naked, winded, and bewildered.

"It's all my fault. I did try to—I tried to touch her, for a second. I'm sorry, Tessa. I saw, and I thought you wanted me to see. I wanted to touch, just for a second."

"I did want you to see," Tessa confesses. "Because I could see you and Robbie. And it was so hot."

Silence.

She says what all of us are thinking. What all of us were wanting.

"It was, sweetie." Robbie smiles half-heartedly.

"I wrecked it." I'm an idiot. A very horny idiot. I pull my shirt from the floor and cover my chest, huddling up. "Do you forgive me? Or will you? Someday?"

"You're totally forgiven! There was no hard, fast rule. I—um, I'm pretty sure my hand was on Robbie's leg at one point. I didn't think it was bad."

Leo turns his head from his knees to look woefully at Robbie. He doesn't speak, just stands up. Tessa hastily tosses him his pants and he startles as he suddenly realizes he's the only one not covered up. He pulls them in front of his waist and tips his head toward the living room.

Robbie nods back. He follows him out of the bedroom.

Tessa and I climb back on the bed, side by side. "How do you live with him? Mr. Nonverbal Communication?"

"I like it." She smiles. "He talks when it matters. He always listens, too. How do you live with Mr. PDA?"

Okay, so Robbie has no shame in the sense of making a fool of himself for love. He will interrupt a college class to bring me a sugar cookie (with one bite missing), starts every session of Skin Deep with a mushy dedication to "The love of my life, Charlotte" and spouts poetry at random intervals. I eat that stuff up. Tessa would live in constant mortification at the attention it draws to her. I've seen Leo give her a public "shout out" once, which consisted of a long slow nod as he pointed a drumstick at her before he started to play. Tessa nearly fainted.

I shrug. "Our dudes are different. We're different."

"I like that. I like that we're different," Tessa exclaims emphatically. "This vacation is a chance to be totally different. To try new things and... see new things."

"I'm pretty sure we both saw a lot."

This is serious. It's the completely wrong time to giggle. Naturally, we both giggle.

That's why we're best friends.

"Leo's possessive. I like that. Being the nerd growing up, the shy girl growing up—I was the girl no one wanted. The way he wants me and thinks I'm worth going crazy over? I love that."

"I know. I didn't mean to cross a line."

"You didn't. You wouldn't have. Look, Robbie caused us all kinds of good feelings by biting us. Touching us. Touch can be affectionate and not sexual."

"Um, I'm pretty sure this touch was going to be sexual."

"Well... that's because we're sharing pleasure. Maybe we just need a little more space for sharing. Ways to touch that aren't so intimate," Tessa suggests.

It's on the tip of my tongue to argue that we have crossed so many lines and boundaries, and any definition of intimate has left town. But Tessa is the smartest one in our little messed up "pack," so I'm willing to listen.

She chews her lip. "I should talk to Leo first."

"Good plan."

I TENTATIVELY CROSS into the living room, unsure of what I'll see.

Broken bones?

Overturned furniture?

Black eyes?

Nope.

Our guys are doing some sort of Vulcan mind meld, hands on the back of each other's necks, eyes closed as they stand forehead to forehead with half-grimaces on their faces.

"Uh—"

"Shh." Tessa waves me to silence.

Too late. We broke whatever it was.

Leo looks up slowly. He smiles his usual easy grin. "Words got harder after I got bitten."

"You weren't terribly generous with 'em in the first place," Robbie jokes.

Good. Joking is good. I breathe a little easier.

"That's why I picked you for the front man. I needed someone with a big mouth." Leo gives the smack right back.

The balance in the universe is restored.

"Come here." Tessa swoops over, now in one of the hotel's plush robes, and steals Leo off to their room.

Robbie and I wave as the door shut firmly and crash into each other in relief.

"Handsy little thing, aren't you?" he laughs into my hair.

"Don't tease me."

"I'm not."

I glare.

"Okay, I was," he sheepishly admits.

"Are you two good now?" I ask, referring to the explosion and then fizzle we witnessed.

"Yeah, very good." Robbie taps his head. "His demon... the part that's a wolf—can speak to whatever's in me, if we just get it quiet enough. Not words, exactly. Something you can sense. That's why we hunt together. We're in rhythm." Robbie's hips do a deep thrust that I don't think he even notices. "I can feel him running in me now."

"Tessa, too?"

"All of you. All three of you. A banquet for my demon, a feast for my soul."

I told you he was a poet.

So, it occurs to me that Robbie had a different set of needs met, a different set of completion. He was connected in a physical way to all three of us. He was enjoying the show, but he already had his "hands-on" (fangs-on?) time. I wanted more closeness, but if you think I would ever sleep with someone else, you're crazy.

Have my finger inside Tessa while Leo's fucking her, so I can feel them moving together? That seems fine. Completely. And amazingly, orgasmically hot.

There is something wrong with me. I know, I know.

"What's wrong, Babe?"

Okay, so "I know" was not exactly a truthful statement.

"I don't know. I don't want to go around couple swapping, but I wouldn't mind touching them while they're going at it, and I wouldn't mind them touching us, either. If that makes me some kind of sex fiend, so be it. I wouldn't ever do it unless you're on board! I thought we were on board." I sink onto the couch where we'd been all tangled up an hour ago, inhaling each other, touching, reaching... I reached too far.

Robbie joins me. "I'm on board."

"Yeah, well, I fell off the damn ship." I rubbed my wrist. Leo's strong, but I'm strong, too. He didn't do any damage, but the grasp of his hand hurt my heart more than my body. I betrayed his trust, and they just gave the supreme act of trust to my Robbie, my everything.

"He's afraid."

"Huh?"

"Of losing Tessa to someone like you or me. Someone who can't infect her."

"He can't infect her unless he bites her during the three wolf moons," I gasp. "I'd never, ever—" I'm so angry I'm sputtering. "I would *never*! They're—they're *us*! They're the couple that beats everything and stays together, they're the version of us that can get married, grow old, and have kids! I want the best for them. I wouldn't steal her."

Hurt crosses his face. Apology crosses mine. We move on. We'll beat everything, too. It'll just look different.

"I wouldn't steal her, either. You know how he said it's gotten harder for him to communicate after getting bitten? Tessa doesn't need the words to understand him. She's powerful. She can reach right inside him and see it all. But to Leo, he's still shortchanging her when she's got that ruddy big brain, and all those degrees will pile up after her name. He'll have 'em, too. He just got the wind up and overreacted, that was all."

I can see that. Leo loves her like I love Robbie. The "live and die for" kind of love. So it makes sense that anyone invading their union is scary.

But.

"But when you were biting Tessa, he was touching her and looking right at me. He wanted me to get turned on." Or I have a dirty, maliciously sexual brain that wants to believe that.

"Noticed that. Not so much about you being turned on, but about showing you. Wolves show dominance that way."

"Come again?"

"Very bloody soon, I hope," he grumbled but continued. "Alpha wolves show dominance by keeping the mate of their choice for themselves. Wolves don't steal off alone if they want to get down to it. They nuzzle and lick and all that in front of other pack members, but the other members can't mate with either of the alphas."

"Where the hell did you learn all this?"

"Partly from Leo, partly from *BBC Earth*. The point is that Leo wants you and me to be in his pack, but he doesn't want us to touch his mate. He definitely doesn't want us to mate with her."

"This is very creepy. I don't like thinking of Leo in terms of animalistic behavior without his normal sarcastic genius behind it."

"It's still there, babes. Don't worry. We sorted it out. We both liked the show, not just any show, this show, with the people we trust. Touches are probably all right, too, but make sure you ask permission. That goes double for him."

"How does that go double for him?" I roll my eyes.

His hands are suddenly on me, one tangling the fine gold chain adorning my neck around his fingers, twisting the emerald up into his palm as he pulls me closer, the other indenting the back of my neck. "Because you're the future Mrs. Scarsdale, and you're mine. I bit you. I proposed to you. You said yes. Vampires mate for life and so do wolves.

We can do whatever we want—but you still belong to me. An' I belong to you."

I shiver as his hands and lips turned into cool velvety kisses and touches, bringing me astride him.

I belong to you. You belong to me, too.

"I love you."

"I love you, too."

"We both love you *both*. Wanna see our room?"

I almost fall off Robbie's lap, but vampire reflexes are insane. Like, if Robbie could play basketball as a pro (but there are afternoon games, buses with big windows, daytime flights, etc.) he would be the NBA's highest-paid player.

Clumsily sitting up after my near collision with the carpet, I turn to see Tessa and Leo smirking from the doorway of their room.

I believe I offered that same invitation a while ago.

Why will this time be any different?

Oh, well. When in Rome...

This is Sin City. Let's gamble.

"YOU HAVE A *jacuzzi*?! When were you going to tell us?" Robbie demands as we follow our friends into their room.

"Um. Right after we got on the flight home?" Tessa admits, abashed.

I thought it was strange that they didn't use the main bathroom located between the two bedrooms. I see why now. Their bedroom has its own bathroom that could swallow up the other one. The jacuzzi is deep and sunken, lined with ledges that must act as benches. It is surrounded by mirrors and large ledges for candles (or sitting on for various positions, my inner naughty girl reminds me). There's a long marble vanity with two sinks, a toilet and a bidet, and a stall shower that is triple the length of the one in our room.

"So..." Tessa is shy. I mentioned that. She stands next to Leo and bends down to turn the tub on. There's a timer on the wall. "What do we think? An hour? Or ninety minutes?"

"Ninety." Leo goes to the wall and plays with a dimmer switch. The lights are low, but everything is clearly visible. "There. We can see better."

"There's more space. You guys can have this side, we'll have this one." Tessa gestures to the benches. She might have been arranging couples at a dinner party.

"Hands to ourselves—or ask first," Robbie clarifies, hand protectively on my hip.

Leo nods quietly. In a gesture that surprises me, he comes over and puts his forehead to mine.

I'm not demon enough to "communicate" like that.

But there's something in me. I can't hear words. I feel something. Pain. Sadness. Images. They create a sentence in my thoughts.

Sorry. I was wrong. I hurt my pack.

"I hurt the pack, too," I whisper, hugging him impulsively. He hugs me back.

His hands linger, not because he's breaking his own rules, but because suddenly, we're back in that tangled-up sandwich that started us on this path. Tessa and Robbie are squeezed in, there's nuzzling and cheeks are kissed, and there's suddenly skin. Lots and lots of skin.

Towels and robes drop. The lights are low and yellow, showing off everything. Naked bodies are pressing. Tessa's pert, rounded tits rub against my own bigger, fuller set. Robbie's cock is against my thigh while Leo's hands are still on my back.

It's a sensory overload of the best kind. I hug everyone I can reach, hug them harder than ever, all the different textures and tones making the most beautiful mosaic for my tingling fingers.

Everyone else is doing the same.

That's just the way everyone seems to want it. Tessa steps back first and very deliberately wraps her fist around Leo's thick hardness, pumping him until his eyes close.

It's like a dance. I know the steps I'm supposed to take next. I wrap my hand around Robbie's throbbing, cool erection, and squeeze.

"This isn't exactly fair," Tessa remarks in a musing tone.

"What isn't?"

"We can't use the mirrors to our advantage. Robbie doesn't reflect."

I let out a sigh of relief. "We'll change positions if you need a different angle," I chuckle.

"Ditto," Leo agrees.

There's no sound but the rumble of jets and thunder of flowing water. We all realize what we just agreed to and what we're about to do. It was a rushed, fumbling fantasy being acted out before, and now it's deliberate.

"Ladies first," Robbie murmurs, kissing my shoulder and guiding me into the tub.

Tessa joins me, and we sit, curled up on respective sides like nymphs on rocks, waiting for our men to wade through the water and claim us in front of hungry eyes.

Part Three: Third Act

"You know, they say couples focus too much on each other. They need hobbies with other couples." Robbie breaks the tension.

"We could bowl," Leo replies, completely straight-faced.

"Ballroom dancing," Tessa giggles.

"*Bedroom* dancing," I suggest, and the tension is back in place, but it's more friendly. "I've never done it in a hot tub."

"We haven't, either."

"What? You didn't break this puppy in?" Robbie steps in. His cock is out and up, pointing straight toward me like some sort of homing beacon, white and smooth, a marble phallus that no Renaissance master would have dared to carve.

Some women don't like sucking cock. I guess it depends on whose cock it is. Robbie's is so perfect and so delicious (at least to me) that not giving it some attention is a crime. When he sits, I disappear.

Under the water. On my knees.

Underwater blow jobs take practice. I come up wet and coughing, gagging and wiping my eyes. "So not sexy," I choke out.

"But I appreciate the thought, Char," Robbie says genuinely, thumping me on the back, pushing my hair back as I blink.

"That's what these are for," Leo sits on the ledge that's out of the water. Tessa grins and slips over to him smoothly. She looks up at him, eyes sparkling.

"Can I?" she asks eagerly.

"You only," Leo sighs as she tucks her hair behind her ear and then devours him.

Robbie moans and whimpers and flat-out winces because he's been on the verge of cumming for ages now. I let out a little gasp of my own. Watching Tessa worship Leo is not just hot in a kinky way that my brain has decided is perfectly fine for a limited time only (or not). It's also inspiring.

"That looks like a good idea. Let me try this again." I slink back between Robbie's legs as he shifts himself onto the edge of the tub. I practically inhale him, this time without the un-sexy gasping and water up the nose.

At first, I'm too lost in listening to him to notice anything else. I love hearing him moan my name, gasp, and hit the high notes. Behind us, Leo whispers little praises and grunts softly, but no less intensely.

After a few minutes, I notice what the warm water does to Robbie's body. See, I dated him before he got sick. Back before it was a choice of dying from cancer and staying dead or dying from a vampire's bite and getting up the next night. He's my first and only lover, which is just fine with me. Anyway, I love him now, I loved him then.

Submerged in a hot tub, the steamy room and beyond body temp water circulating over his legs from the knees down- it warms him up. For a second, it's like he's alive again.

"Baby, are you okay?" Robbie pushed me back from my treat for the second time that night. Behind us, reflected in the mirror, I see Leo's face lose its blissful expression.

"I'm great," I say, and I mean it. He's still here.

I wish he hadn't had to... change.

He smells salt. That's what he once said when I told him it was annoying that he could tell if I'd been crying. Right now, he immerses himself in the water to grab me and hold me close. "If this is too far, we'll go back to our room. This isn't—"

"I'm not misty about that!" I whisper. In fact, if I'd just kept my eyes on the glass behind Robbie's shoulder, I would be lost in the study of another insanely hot couple doing delectable things to each other. But I'm not looking there right now.

"Tell me?"

"You feel... human." It's one reason I love shower sex. The chill (which I have no problem with) leaves, and I pretend that we'll never have to make a hard choice, one that fully mortal couples never consider.

"I *am* human. I just tore the sell-by label off my packet. Be here for you as long as you need me, precious."

I laugh and sniff in. "I know. Sorry. I didn't mean to-"

"What's wrong?" Tessa's voice has a note of alarm, a clarion call to action. She turns and gasps when she sees my head down, cradled under Robbie's, tears mixing with the sheen the steam leaves on my cheeks. "Why is Charlotte crying? Leo! Why didn't you stop me? Why are you crying? Robbie, why is she crying?" she demands, frantic bursts of questioning like the yips of a hyper terrier.

"'Cause I didn't know what to do and you felt too good to interrupt," Leo says honestly, sliding back in the water as well.

I think it's instinctive. Tessa has held me while I've cried angry tears over junior high crushes and Lumberjack losses at the state finals, sad tears when I thought I was going to lose Robbie to cancer, or when my dad couldn't make it to my high school graduation. Big tears or little tears, Tessa has one setting, "Hug Charlotte."

I love Tessa.

Tessa has one setting on a lot of things, which is why she'll go far. She refuses to be derailed from her objective.

Even if her objective is me, naked in the arms of my also nude, hard boyfriend.

I know I should be reveling in the comforting words that both of them are murmuring to me, rocking me in this lovely, bubbly warm cradle. I am, I promise.

I'm also having some sort of brain-gasm, where all I can think about is how I'm in the middle of an amazing sandwich. Behind me are soft, round tits with hard nipples and goddess-like red hair, and in front of me is a guy who would put the entire cast of Chippendale's out of work just by taking off his shirt.

The earlier hug was wonderful, but this feels different after a few minutes. The soothing words stop. Leo moves behind Tessa. I don't know if I expect him to pull her away or hug me, too.

He goes for a combination. He tugs Tessa back a bit and that gives him room to get in and add another layer to this sandwich. "Sad?"

"Not anymore. Thanks, guys."

"Touch is healing. I read it on a teabag," Leo deadpans and cautiously opens his arm.

Robbie tucks me under it, putting his other arm around Tessa. We've made a life ring, each guy has his arm around each girl, our arms around each guy, while Tessa and I face each other. It's extremely intimate.

I can see everything. Feel everything, if I let my hands wander. As one, we squeeze in a little tighter, four heads brushing, smiles soft or vanishing. All of us are inches away from having body parts brush someone else's, while still being connected to our own sweetheart.

Looking is good. Some part of me wants even more. But there are boundaries we shouldn't cross—without permission.

My voice is the one that breaks the silence. I know they're all supporting me, and I want them to know it worked. "Touch is good." I squeeze Robbie's hip and Leo's shoulder.

Robbie steps back a bit, hand kneading my cheek under the water. He's still got his wrist carelessly draped over Tessa's shoulder. "Wish we had a camera right about now." Robbie admires the view. "Leo, we've got the greatest beauties on earth. Two in one place, it's an effing miracle."

Tessa moves back next, freeing herself from Robbie's arm to raise her own. She toasts the guys with an imaginary glass. "The greatest stud muffins, ever. Shoot. I should have ordered more champagne."

"Champagne in a hot tub. Aren't we living the high life?" I manage to chuckle. That's what they want, what I want, happiness restored. Honestly, a girl from Pine Ridge shouldn't get so hung up over a pulse. "Or the high *un-life*. You see what I did there?"

I have no one to blame but myself for the sudden over-the-head splash Robbie gives me.

I splash him back, though. Even though sometimes I'm sad he's different, I'm always thrilled he's still here.

I'm sure Leo will be too reserved to join in this splash fest and will shortly give us a one-word reminder to chill. Probably the actual word, "Chill."

So, I'm surprised when he mutters, "That's not fair. You're bigger than her." (Robbie is bigger than him, too.)

"What are you—argh! Leo!"

Leo dunks him casually, one hand shoving him under as his leg sweeps behind Robbie's knees. Robbie bobs right back up and hits the water hard with both palms, drenching Leo's auburn hair. Leo's normally stoic facade break into a comic snorting and snuffling fit.

It's on. Tessa and I squeal and stand back as the warm water flies in all directions, mostly aiming at those two handsome faces.

"Guys!" Tessa finally giggles. "Don't make me witch-out."

"No, please witch-out," Robbie laughs and splutters, wiping his face. "Show me what you've got!"

Tessa says something and strikes the water, and suddenly it's taller than us, and towering over us, spinning us, but we're not exactly submerged. It's like a water slide with a funnel, and I love those. I scream and Robbie screams and Leo laughs and grabs her.

"This is the best vacation ever!" Tessa cries, happy and free, naked, and powerful in the forces she controls.

And so hot. Leo thinks so, too. Robbie and I giggle and kiss, and exchange a look as we sweep around again. "Quite the show."

"Amazing," I gasp.

Leo growls and grabs Tess even closer, arm around her possessively. She moans. I would never have guessed it, but she likes the brawn side of him as much as the brains. "Leo, please? Like this?"

He runs a hand over her throat, stopping at her breast and squeezing hard. "But they..."

"They don't mind. They wanna share. Share the view. We'll share. We'll both show, right?"

"Yes," I answer first, breathless and nodding.

Leo looks more at me than at Robbie and pushes Tessa toward me for a second, following her over until we're in the life ring huddle again. "I won't touch!" I swear. "Except for hugs. Hugs are good?" I squeak, suddenly worried he's mad at me for being so eager.

"Talking time," he grunts and looks at Robbie.

Robbie and he move to one side, their heads bowing. They don't use words. That freaks me out and makes me jealous of how they connect, just by letting their demonic forces or essences communicate somehow in the intense silence, broken only by rapid breathing and rushing water. I can't do that. They're what I'd call first-generation demons. They have all that demonic energy and power in them, right at the surface. I have some in me somewhere, but it's nothing like that, a trickle to their raging river.

I like being normal, but when everyone else in your closest circle of friends has really moved over to the "supernatural" category in a big way and you haven't, you feel a little lost and left behind. I'd love another hug right now, but the talking time isn't quite done.

"Ah." Robbie nods when he steps back.

We separate again, couples paired off. Robbie's lips press my ear and my neck. "Do you realize *what* you'll be showing him? He wants to make sure you and Tessa get it. This is... intimate. Parts of you and pieces of you and emotions you can't hide. Raw and naked in whole different ways."

Which shouldn't excite me. But it does. I think I need to call a moratorium on should and shouldn't, at least in Vegas. "It's okay. I trust them."

Leo's voice is a rumble in Tessa's ear that I can't make out, but he talks to Tessa urgently. She looks at me a long time, then Robbie. She blushes. "Well... he saw me already."

"This is different. Not just acting out the urges together. This is showing. On purpose. Watching." Tessa's thighs clench hard. Leo nuzzles her hair. "Tessa says okay. We can leave if we want privacy. Or it's too much."

"Too much bloody *waiting*." Robbie rubs against my cheek again, hard tip nudging pointedly, seeking a haven. "Together or separate, can we please get on with it?"

"The *dead* guy is impatient?" Leo smiles crookedly.

"So is the very alive girlfriend." I bump back against him. I know we need space to keep separate, but I miss the proximity. It's more exciting when we're so close we can reach out and touch them. I want to help with those safe, cozy feelings, and also the intense, mind-numbing pleasurable feelings, the almost-but-not-quite-line-crossing feelings.

Like Robbie gets to. He made Leo and Tessa high on pleasure and all I did was cause a huge bump in this otherwise orgasmic road.

I'm officially an adult this weekend. I'm too old to pout.

Robbie loves when I pout.

I spin toward him and my bottom lip is being a stubborn brat and puffing out as I think of what Robbie can do and- oh. Hello.

Ruby eyes rake mine. He's horny and suped up on a tasting menu of powerful blood. "Hey, Baby," I purr. I can't help it if that hungry, almost dangerous look is a turn on.

"Beginning to think you like the other acts in Vegas better than your own personal rockstar," he hisses low, pulling my hands to his hips.

"Nothing further from the truth," I reassure and I'm being totally honest. Watching Leo and Tessa is like the icing on the cake, but Robbie's the entire banquet. I work my fingers beyond hips, down into his glutes, smooth, perfect muscles that indent slightly under my fingers.

"Sure?" his tone is teasing. He play-mocks me with a pout of his own. "'Cause your lower lip says otherwise."

"You're too sexy when you pout. I can't think," I fuss, looking at the deep red eyes and the fangs that somehow remind me more of a jungle beast than anything evil. Just primal. I have questions about the primal nature, suddenly. Fortunately, we packed an expert. "Leo?"

Leo unlocks his lips from Tessa's long enough to go, "Hm?"

"Do packs mate at the same time? Members of the packs. In *proximity*?"

Robbie's hand is hard on my hip, digging in.

"Not usually. Alphas show off. Not so much the others."

"But we're a hybrid pack," Robbie's voice is a growl, more guttural as it works past razor-sharp canines, so sharp they only sting for a second when they slip in. "Vampires, witches, werewolves, and part-demons. Two alphas, different breeds." I feel his fingers push between my thighs and dig in and up with just a touch of roughness. Robbie wants my mind back on him.

It's superglued. I lean forward with a gasp as two fingers invade, hard and fast, digging for a kernel of flesh that he never fails to find inside me. My hands slam onto the porcelain ledge and I look into the mirror surrounding it. It's fogged with steam and covered in remnants of splashes. Robbie doesn't reflect, but I can feel him, his tip pushing at my entrance, his hands on my back, sliding up to grip my shoulders.

With a nudge, my knees make their way onto the bench seat we vacated, my rump and the split of my pink pussy now on display above the water. Since I have Mr. Absence of Reflection behind me, I can see-well, I can see a lot. His cock is going in and out of my pussy, but his cock doesn't reflect, either. Do you get the picture?

Tessa did.

Everything is on display, open and pink, wet, and spreading. My cheeks are hot, my whole body is hot and for a second I think about saying we need to turn around or leave.

Then Tessa whimpers and paws frantically at Leo's bicep. "That's like—oh God, what's the word I want?"

"Erotic," Leo supplies. His chest is rising and falling harder than it was seconds ago.

Which it is, watching my soft pink folds spread and spasm on nothing, glimpses of my inner walls flashing. I *do* feel more naked and vulnerable than ever in my life, but it's... it's not bad.

"Erotic doesn't cover it. Fuck me, too, right now, right now." Tessa flings herself up onto him like she has wings to lift her. Part of me wonders if the water magically pushed her up or the air, or if Tessa did manage to learn flying spells. (She tried the whole broom thing once. Ran into a nasty flock of Canadian geese.)

"That's the ticket," Robbie hisses as Leo collapses against their side of the mirrored wall. Because both sides have mirrors, we get to watch them too, the thick, heavy rod that splits Tessa open and the way her walls cling around it. She bounces on him, head thrown back, breasts lifting as her arms reach back and wrap passionately with Leo's, some Celtic knot of pulsing limbs and pounding hips.

"Ohh." I lost words one peep show ago.

"Not gonna last. This is too bloody good." Robbie's forehead hits my shoulder as he arches over me.

"I'm almost there."

"Almost isn't gonna—shit..."

I know that noise and the sudden jackhammer speed of his hips. There's one thing that works when our speeds are mismatched. "Drinks are on me," I whisper.

I KNOW I'M SCREAMING. My brain and my body are on a high and words are back on vacation. Blood is rushing out of my neck, which is pulled back into Robbie's mouth. His arm is around my waist and his spurting cock is still inside me, no worries about protection anymore.

"Shit!" Tessa shrieks and whimpers and slams her hips down. Robbie and I are breathing hard (not that he *needs* to, but it's a habit) as we wait to see their big finish.

It's impressive. She reaches down and furiously rubs her clit as Leo yanks her back and shoves his mouth over her pulse point sucking, growling, and worrying the skin. There's something of the animal with the kill in the gesture, but I get why in a second.

"Ooooh!" Tessa moans and leans back, limp, whimpering. Leo cums in her so hard, thrusting so forcefully, that we see her pink, flushed mound twitch from pelvic bone out. As soon as he empties in her, Leo gathers her up in his arms, spins her around, and buries his forehead in her neck, shoulders heaving.

"Good. Good, lover. Leo, it was perfect," she soothes.

"Not too rough?" he whispers, sounding genuinely fearful.

"No!"

The heat has layers. Still tingling, still throbbing, and shaking from the onslaught of sexual energy I just shared with Robbie, I can still feel other things. Worry. Fear. Comfort.

The big tough guy still worries. I exchange a look with Robbie. "Should we go?" I whisper.

"No!" Tessa frantically shakes her head. She shares a small smile with me. "That was so amazing. I'm not—I'm not into girls, but um—um... That was hot."

"I know!" I enthuse. "You guys... You guys are perfect together." I hit the word "perfect" hard, trying to make Leo look up, and come back to us.

"Budge up," Robbie sighs and pushes me out of his lap and gently nudges Tessa away from Leo, both of them jumping as his hand touches her breast for a second. Leo hisses, but before he can do more, Robbie rams his forehead to his.

Again, with the being heterosexual thing, but our two guys in kissing distance, are fucking *gorgeous*. If Robbie wasn't mine and Leo wasn't Tessa's, I would pay money to see how this movie could end.

Robbie doesn't smooch him (that's not their thing, so I'm relieved) but he does make a purring, growling sound I had thought was reserved for me. Leo makes a soft grunt, eyes stubbornly downcast. Another, louder purr and rumble, Leo finally looking up. Stunning the crap out of me, Robbie sniffs in hard and puts his hand on Tessa's hip.

Great. My boyfriend is going to lose an arm. I'm pretty sure even a vampire doesn't grow that back. I'm completely *sure I don't want to find out. Also, hello, hip-grabbing? Without* me? *No fair, dude.*

Leo pulls back and smiles, relief evident on his face. "Really?"

"Without a doubt."

"It's so rude of them to talk behind our backs. Or in front of them." Tessa folds her arms sternly.

"Sorry, Tess," Leo murmurs, spooning behind her, touching her gently all over, as if putting her pieces in order.

"What did you say?" I hiss as Robbie snuggles me in turn.

"That he made his mate happy, made her feel safe and loved. That his strength makes her feel hot, puts her in heat. She's not afraid. She can handle him." Robbie's eyes meet Tessa's suddenly. She smiles and mouths, "Thank you." "She's strong, our girl. But she's not a patch on *my* girl."

"We have to stop this eventually, right?" Tessa moans as Leo's lips tenderly trace the spot where he clamped down hard.

"In time to catch our flight at least."

"And eat," Leo mumbles.

"You lot have to eat. I brought my snacks." Robbie winks, catching my elbow for his crass remark, even though there's no harm in it.

Tessa's breath hitches suddenly. Leo's head raises, nostrils flared.

Robbie's head lifts, too. "What can you possibly smell in here with all this water?" I demand.

"Arousal."

"Ah." Makes sense. There's probably a metric ton of it pouring out of me alone.

"Tessa likes when you snack. I liked it, too. We— we saw what happened when you bit Charlotte." Leo stretches casually and moves them closer to him. "Is it better during?" he asks me.

Well, I can't lie to my very best friends! "Only about a thousand times better. B-but it's fine without that. I mean—" My panic kicked in. Are they—do they—want to have sex with him now? We were super clear on that *not* being an option!

"If we were close enough..." Tessa bites her lip nervously, looking like she used to look at the third slice of chocolate cake before the great barfing incident, "could you bite us while we were...you know?"

"Can I taste you while you and Leo are coupled up?" Robbie's red irises take over seamlessly. That's a loud yes, even if he sounds hesitant.

"You'd have to be really close." I lick my lips. I like them being really close. "Side-by-side. Or chest-to-chest.

Silence.

"Bed?" Robbie asks, sounding tight, those uneven, unnecessary shallow breaths returning.

"The tub," Tessa says quickly. She mutters something and the water is sparkling clean, back to normal water level (pre-splash fest) and the timer is back to start. "Easy cleanup. Are you sure you don't mind?" Her eyes rake over both of ours.

"Yes, that's fine." So fine. *Sweetheart gets a treat. And I get to watch.*

"My heart belongs to Lottie. My fangs are available on occasion." He traces a hand over my chest.

Funny, I'd gotten comfortable with the fact that our bodies were bare. They were all different, and all attractive in different ways. My brain tried to nudge at my curiosity, asking if I'd like to get more up close and personal with those bodies across the tub. Try out that thicker, stockier cock, slip my fingers inside of Tessa's tunnel and feel her clamp down.

The answer is coming back as no. I like sharing, but I didn't like the idea of coming *between*. Sharing somehow had to have equal compartments.

"You don't mind, babes?" Robbie brushes his hardness against me again.

"No! I just don't—ooh." The question I'd had, which was 'what will I be doing' was now answered. I was going to get pounded from behind, again.

"Love to love you face to face, pet, but I'm trying to maneuver across three bodies." Robbie moves to the center of the tub, keeping me impaled on him, the fullness widening me past our normal as he moved me with him, bringing me smack into Tess and Leo. "Ah. Hang on a mo."

Tessa grips my shoulders suddenly, rocking forward. From her wince switching to a blissful expression, I guess Leo also had lightning-quick recovery time.

"This is new." Tessa let out a gasp as she collides and we jostles, the guys finding their stroke. The side effect that the guys didn't seem to notice right away was that they were bumping and grinding us into one another.

A lot.

Well, you know, side effects are rarely this nice, so I might as well enjoy it. Tessa's breasts are so soft, I just want to reach out and grab them, but having them rubbing all across my larger set is also awesome.

I suddenly understand the reason Robbie is constantly grabbing onto mine.

I meet her eyes. Her mouth is slightly open, pink skin going pinker. If Robbie is going to give them something to get off on, I might as well do my part, right? I arch my back. Leo briefly meets my eyes as my nipples bounce against Tessa's sort of on purpose. She gulps in air and lets out a moan. Leo's hand inserted itself between us and tugged her nipples hard, the perfect stroke that she seemed to prefer. I don't know if he realizes it—I know it wasn't on purpose, but this meant the rougher skin on the back of his knuckles was rubbing my sensitive nipples, too.

No one has ever touched those but Robbie. My body tenses up, my stomach knots in a nervous way, and then a good way. It wasn't on purpose. It wasn't like Leo wanted to touch anyone other than Tess. I didn't move back.

Robbie, on the other hand, surges forward, driving Leo and Tessa back to the edge of the tub, knocking them back to the ledge. "Leo. Arm."

"Her first. It'll make me cum. She has to go first," Leo rasps, shoving Tessa's arm up, over my shoulder.

"God, I love this." I can't help letting out a moan as Tessa's arm and Robbie's head meshed with my neck and shoulders in the middle. They sat, and we were leaning over. I love all the closeness and the power, etc., etc. but I didn't have supernatural balance. "Whoa!"

I pitch forward and Robbie's arm goes around my waist more tightly. Leo grabs my shoulder as Tess keeps posting on him. We were all supporting each other in this incredible net of sex and steam. I didn't need a bite to get off again, but I couldn't wait to watch Tessa let go because of it.

"EASY, TESS, HOLD ONTO Lottie. Leo, hold onto her hips." Robbie's speech is broken as he licks a trail across my cheek and neck to land on the soft white skin of Tessa's arm.

I manage to turn my head in time to watch the fangs slip out and the dark red eyes gleam. Fuck, to me that's so hot. There are so many sides to hot on this guy. Then, he lunges in and pins her arm against me. Leo grunts. Tessa screams in the best possible way.

"I'm cumming! I'm cumming, I'm cumming, I'm cumming, Leo!"

"I can feel it. God, that pussy gets tight when he's in you. Biting you."

Does Leo realize how that sounds?

Erotic as hell, in a good way. "You next," I tell him with a wink.

"Ladies first." Robbie lifts his head and swallows several times. "I like my heavy drink at the end of the meal."

"Are you calling me fat?" Leo asks, perfectly deadpan.

"No. Thick. Heavy. Powerful. So powerful."

"Fuck, Robbie, fix me." I yank on Leo's arm, which had two consequences. It unbalances us and I flail my hands, clasping hard on Tessa's as she tries to catch me. Robbie bit me in one second and Leo the next. He's never that short and sharp with me. I guess he was overwhelmed, trying to take care of everyone at once.

My man always comes through.

Speaking of coming through, something else is coming through me, something I have never felt. No, I'm not talking about, "Ooh, I've never had semi-group sex before," or "Ooh, I'm having a lesbian awakening." No, this is a literal, physical sensation.

Power. Electricity, heat, and blinding pleasure, a tourniquet in my pussy that spreads up my ribcage and squeezes my heart until I'm afraid I'm having a heart attack. It was a blur. I was cumming, Tessa was cumming again (or still on the first one), our palms pressed together so that I felt every tremor and gasp like it was in my own body, I could feel

Robbie tightening and Leo's eyes were unfocused, and black, his teeth grit and growling long and loud.

"Yes! *Yes*!" I let out a scream that came from the toes up.

Then the world went bright white.

"HONEY?" ROBBIE ASKS, leaning back against a porcelain tub that's now got impact marks in it like it was hit by a human boulder. Two impacts, actually, one on either side. (One is smaller and more Leo-shaped.)

"Hmmm?" My voice is high and tight.

"What the bloody fuck was that?"

"I..." I don't know.

"Lottie's part demon," Leo pulls himself up and hoists Tessa, still shaking and gasping, against his chest.

Robbie frowns, eyes narrowing. "We know. In all the times we've made love, she's never—"

"I think I know. I think I *know*!" gasps Tessa.

The way she says it, looking at me with bright, expectant eyes rings a bell.

We've had this conversation since I was eleven. Tessa is a witch. Pure and simple. We knew other people, what they were, under the shiny surface of human. We didn't know what I was, and Mom still doesn't get it. Dad has never said more than six words about it— "You get it from my side." There are dozens of different types of demons that look pretty much human or are at least compatible with humans. As the years passed and I didn't develop any unusual characteristics, we shrugged and laughed it off, calling me a mutt, a hybrid, and leaving it at that.

Now, Tessa thinks she's got it. I think I know what she's going to say, but I have no idea how to feel about it.

"You're part succubus," Tessa cries. "You took sexual power, and it did something to you. Since we're all a little bit extra, it did something to us, too. Something very good." She pauses and grins widely, then claps her hand over her mouth. "Oh my God, do I still have all my teeth?"

"Let me check?" Leo turns her head to his and kisses her.

"Lottie? Babes?" Robbie climbs out after me.

I'm running to our room, a towel flung hastily over my shoulders. My fingers are shaking as I dig through my bag and come up clutching my phone.

My knees give out as I sit on the bed, afterglow ruined, mind spinning. Robbie comes and sits beside me, hand on my knee as the phone rings and rings.

"Dad? It's an emergency. Call me back."

"SWEETIE? ARE YOU HURT? Is it your mother? Where are you?"

My dad rarely stays in touch, but when he does, he does the full parenting thing. Right now, he sounds like he would jump on a plane, bail me out of jail, or beat up the guy who broke my heart.

Pretty good for ten seconds, right?

"I'm not hurt, but I'm not okay." My voice won't stop trembling. Robbie rubs me all over, trying to warm me up, but hello, no body temperature to speak of, so not entirely helpful.

"What happened? Is it the Drysdale boy?"

"Scarsdale, Daddy, and no. Well, yeah. In a way. Dad, what am I?"

A pause. "What?"

"Don't BS me this time. Don't rush off. Don't put it off. I'm older and it matters now, for real. People I care about could get hurt if I don't know stuff. So, tell me. What *am* I? What are *you*?"

The sigh speaks volumes. "Let me get a beer."

I wait for the beer. I hear noises in the hotel bathroom. Tessa is witching up the damages, bless her. When Dad comes back on, he sounds tired. Not like Mr. Fun, the guy I usually chat with on random Fridays, holidays, and my birthday, when he remembers.

"I'm part-incubus. Because you're a girl, it means you're technically part-succubus. A succubus is a female demon who—"

"I know what they do." I've killed one before.

I can hear the brakes squealing in your head.

Charlotte! Aside from the undead boyfriend and the kinky sex, we thought you were such a nice, sweet girl!

Right?

I am, I promise. But Pine Ridge isn't always so sweet. Remember when I told you that there are people who make evil an action verb? We can't let those people live in our town. We try to get those nasty ones to leave, the people like Tessa, Leo, and Robbie, the people with that extra power. We can't let the normal locals do it, they wouldn't stand a chance. It's not like there's some organization of secret crime fighters in Pine Ridge. (Or maybe there is. If it's a secret, I wouldn't know, right?) It's more like when you see trash in your town, you pick it up. If you see a killer in your midst, you stop it. This would normally mean calling the police.

Yeah. Right. *"911, there's a shape-shifting sex demon sucking the life out of Mr. Peabody, my gym teacher, who thinks he just got really lucky on LonelyandSingle.com."* That would go over like a ton of lead. So...

So, Mr. Minegold (the nice vampire who helped Robbie), Tess, Leo, and I killed the thing when it turned on us when we tried to save Mr. Peabody. And the rest is history. If there's someone giving demons a bad name (excuse the incredible irony there), we do something about it. Now that Robbie's in the "extra special" club, we can usually let Mr. Minegold sit out.

I'm the thing I killed.

I know. I know there are bad vampires and then there are folks like Robbie. There are bad werewolves and great guys like Leo. I know all that, but right now, I feel sick.

"Say something?"

"I... don't know what to say," I admit.

"This is what drove your mom and me apart. I need sexual energy. A little from a lot of people doesn't hurt. A lot from just one person would kill them. I couldn't do that to her."

But... "When do you start needing to feed?" I whisper.

"Well, usually a few years after sexual maturity. Hrm-rm. When you get your—your special friend."

My dad is going to die of the blood rushing to his face. "Dad, I got my period when I was thirteen. I'm twenty-one! For eight years I never 'fed' on anyone."

Hedging. My dad is such a good hedger, he could win the World Topiary Championships if such a thing exists. "I'm only a quarter-in-cubi. You're an eighth-succubus. You probably wouldn't need to feed at all, really. The human side of you is so much stronger, but if you should ever... Well, you and the Drysdale boy—"

"Scarsdale! Yes, Robbie and I have." And thank God, my knees go weak in a whole different way, thank God, I can't kill him by draining sexual energy from him. He's already dead.

"You'll be fine. Your mother couldn't accept that my 'cheating' on her was a matter of survival."

"How often do you need to feed?"

"Me? A couple of times a month is fine."

Clicking. "Dad. Mom could probably handle some sexual energy sharing a few times a month."

Silence. "It wasn't worth the risk."

"But Dad, you're only a *little bit* demon-y, you didn't need to—"

"Yeah, your mother thought the same thing."

Robbie squeezes my hand. "Let it go, luv. Some men will make an excuse for wandering eyes. I only have eyes for you," he whispers.

"What does that mean, Daddy? I'm never going to be faithful? I *love* Robbie. Robbie and I are engaged. And don't you dare tell Mom, I haven't told her yet!"

"No, honey, listen. You're going to be fine. You have half of what I have. You're going to be *fine*. Your young buck is a lucky man. I just hope he can keep up with you. Now, I can't think of my little girl like this. I— whoo. Lottie, I gotta go do taxes or something hard that erases parts of this conversation. Okay? You can always come to me with problems, but girl things and marriage things... Your mom might be the one to talk to, okay?"

He runs again. Like always. It would have been hard to stay, to control those powers and urges. He ran. "I love you, Dad. Have a great weekend."

He hung up. He didn't wish me a happy birthday. He might've been rattled by the sex part of the conversation. Or it could be the fact that he only remembers half the time.

I lean against Robbie. "You heard."

"I heard. I *am* a lucky fella. I do get a little extra. Look, luv, I like my occasional switch of flavors. You can drain my battery and fill me right back up. You're never gonna hurt me, so get that out of your head. You and I don't want anyone else, but that doesn't mean we won't be close to Tessa and Leo if they want to do this sometimes."

I nod slowly. That's right. I wasn't some slavering sex maniac before today and I won't be one after. I love Robbie and he loves me. We can meet each other's needs. If our friends ever want to pitch in... "Do you think they want to? It's not totally fair. What do they get out of it?"

"Pleasure," Leo's voice calls from the living room.

"Closeness." Tessa comes into the bedroom, standing in the half-open door, clad only in a hotel robe. "And some kind of energy share. I shared my power with you guys in the tub and it's... it's awesome. It's a natural high."

Leo saunters in and slings his arm around her. They come and perch on the loveseat across from the bed.

"Kind of *unnatural*," I mutter. "I always knew there was something stronger and faster in me. I thought I had a high sex drive because I had an awesomely hot, sweet, boyfriend."

"Had!? *Have*. An' I accept full responsibility for that sex drive, babes."

"I almost wish I didn't know! I wondered sometimes, but..."

"You have power, but it doesn't have to change you." Leo's eyes go stern. "I turn into a literal beast. Robbie lost his pulse. If you didn't come at him with a stethoscope or run into me three nights of the month, would you know?"

"No," I whisper, sounding a little tremulous.

"To be fair, sex with you is always amazing, out of control, wild, and wonderful. It didn't change when I had to change. You never changed. You didn't treat me differently when I went from Robbie the Human to Robbie the Vampire. I'm not going see you differently or treat you differently than Charlotte-the-girl-who-doesn't-know-what-sort-of-demon-blood-is-in-her to Charlotte-who-is-part-succubus."

"Look, Pine Ridge is a crazy place. You know there have been times when the residents have had to act." Tessa put her arm around me, coming to sit on the other side of me.

I nod. Like I said, there have been times when the people who know what's going on, people like Leo, Tessa, Robbie, and me, have literally run a bad demon out of town. Or not out of town. Run over. Or run down. Whatever makes it stop hurting the place we call home, we do it, just like you wouldn't let a burglar set up shop in *your* house.

"What's the point?" I ask.

"You are strong and you're helpful. You're good, whatever you are. Getting a title doesn't change you unless you let it. Do you suddenly wanna go jump other guys for their sexual energy? What about Leo?"

"No! *God*, no!" I cry, genuinely horrified. Everyone laughs, my cheeks going bright pink. "No offense." I just had a full monty version of Leo's sexual prowess. He's a ten. But Robbie is a ten gazillion. "Sorry, Leo. That came out in a rude way."

"My ego is deeply bruised," he chuckles, not looking offended in the least as he sprawls back, eyes looking rather sleepy.

"You see? You're not going to turn into some philanderin' trollop because you've got a particular power, any more than I'm going to turn into a fanged murderer or Tess is gonna start lurin' kids into houses made of sweets. Kill the stereotype, sweetheart, not our happy future."

My eyes spring leaks simultaneously. I laugh, reaching for all of them at once, making a dogpile of weepy, relieved hugging. "You guys! You're so smart. And calming. I love you. I mentioned that right?"

"Many times," Robbie whispers into my hair. "Enough worries. It's our weekend away. It's my girl's big birthday. I do believe you just told your old man that we're engaged. That means it's real."

Tessa claps her hands, genuinely excitedly. "Guys! It's night!"

Of all the congratulatory phrases I expected, that wasn't it.

"That happens after day," Leo teases gently.

She ignores him and drags me with her, heading to our suitcases which somehow are still packed. (Not like we got distracted or anything, right?) "I feel like painting the town red. Robbie? Isn't that your favorite color?"

He laughs and plays along. "It is. And..." he joins us at my suitcase and takes out a very daring little red dress that I would never wear in chilly, suburban Pine Ridge, "*no one* can resist the hot blonde in the little red dress. 'Specially not this guy."

"Go suit up. We should at least leave the hotel room once per trip." Leo takes Tessa's hand and pulls her away, so we have some privacy to change.

HE WEARS A SAPPHIRE blue shirt that makes his jaw stand out and his eyes sparkle. He skips the tie but wears the dress pants and buttons his cuffs.

I brush out and blow out my wet hair and slink into the body-hugging dress over black lace underwear. I look like sex and sin and trouble. Robbie looks like the bad boy hottie your mama always warned you about.

We're just two college sweethearts who want to get married someday, who love our besties and would possibly give away our life savings if the Lumberjacks made it to major league status.

"You are going to turn the head of every man in the room. The city," Robbie whistles when I emerge.

"I'm going to have to fight off every female in the *state*," I counter saucily.

We kiss, long and deep. There are no sparks and arcs of electricity, no bodies slammed into walls. "Why did I—" I stop, suddenly frustrated. I don't want to be driven by some lustful power in me. I just want to be *me*.

"We were all connected for a second, that's all. My blood, your blood, their blood, my body in yours, your power connected to Tessa's, Leo's demon talking to mine." He hesitates. "How do you feel? After?"

I think. At first, I felt sick. Now, I feel… alert. Awake. Like I drank five energy shots and bathed in espresso, but without the jitters.

I smile. I felt that way since the first day I met Robbie, but with varying degrees of caffeination. "I feel good. Still, that was over the top."

"Newsflash, when the four of us get together, we can be over the top. We can be over the bloody moon. We are powerful together, whether we've got powers or not. We're powerful 'cause we're..."

"A pack." Leo, looking uncharacteristically debonair in a charcoal gray suit minus tie, greets us as we come into the living room.

"Mate, you gotta stop that," Robbie huffs.

"Werewolf hearing," Leo says with an unapologetic shrug. "Didn't catch all of it. Caught enough. Don't freak. You would have still blown us away no matter what you are."

"That's right!" Tessa swirls out, a cloud of white and silver, a cocktail dress with delicate beads on the bodice that catch the light. She looks like an angel.

She is one, no matter where her powers come from or what the world calls her. Most importantly, she's my best friend.

With the criminally big brain.

"Tess? Do succubi live a long time?"

"They're immortal, like vampires. They can get killed, but they're not going to age and die a natural death. You're not fully a succubus, though."

"That's okay. I'm one-eighth immortal. What do you think, Mr. Scarsdale?" I playfully put my arm through his, blinking back tears. "Are you ready to commit to a one-hundredth anniversary? Maybe even a two-hundredth?"

His eyes sear mine, catch them and hold them. "A one millionth, as long as it's with you."

"Good. Let's go." I put my other arm through Tessa's, and Leo places his arm snugly around her hips. It would be ludicrous to think we could get through the door like that, except that we have Tessa. The door magically expands, and we never even break our stride crossing the threshold.

Like Vegas. This place expanded so many things and opened our eyes to fears and needs, passions, and even identities.

"I don't want to leave this part of the trip behind." I look adoringly at Robbie, gratefully at Tess and Leo. "We don't have to do all the crazy bedroom shenanigans, but I never want to lose this, this *pack*." I give Leo the nod for his simple word that explains so much.

The elevator dings and Tessa stares at it. The doors easily could fit eight of us and the car is empty as we step in. Robbie pushes the button to take us down.

"Sounds good to me. Good, bro?" Leo looks at Robbie.

"Good. We were never going to get rid of each other, anyway. I need your big brain, and you need my big mouth." He smirks.

"Pretty much. Tess?"

"Yes!" she squeals, leaning to me, then on Leo, and flailing her arm around to pat at Robbie's elbow. We all laugh at her gleeful embrace.

The lobby feels like a foreign land, where other people, *normal* people might exist, who never know the secrets and bonds that are right under their noses, passing them on killer heels and polished dress shoes.

The night air is balmy and slightly humid, so much warmer than Pine Ridge. The stars are lost in neon, but they're shining at me in Robbie's deep blue-green eyes.

"Don't suppose you'd care to come on down to the chapel? We could have a little do here, a big, fancy one back home…" he wheedles.

"No. Well, not tonight. That's one thing I don't want to stay in Vegas. Tomorrow morning, I'm calling my mom and we can tell her the good news. Tess, will you be my maid of honor?"

"Yes. Oh my gosh! Yes, *of course*!"

"You're the best man." Robbie addresses Leo as Tess and I squeal and yip, attracting stares from people on their way to gamble the night away.

"I figured." Leo nods back. "Buffets? I could eat an elk."

"He's not kidding," Robbie mutters, setting off more laughter.

"Let the pigging out commence. Just don't eat so much you can't dance."

IT'S PINK AND GOLDEN when we make it back to our suite. The drapes are conveniently shut, for those of us with a major aversion to sunlight.

"I'm beat. And my feet are the size of watermelons." Tessa eases off her strappy white sandals, revealing dance-swollen feet. I guess there are some things witchcraft can't fix—at least not if you keep dancing.

"I need to shower and sleep," Robbie yawns. "Char?"

"Coming."

I am, following him to our room, wondering if later on our bed will hold four instead of two, if I'll link my hands with Tessa and taste the sexual energy of someone else this time, now knowing what it is and what to look for.

I wonder if I'll be like my father, craving for this unnecessary taste to the point where I lose the love of my life- a long life, it looks like.

My bare feet are sore as I touch the cold tile. I sink gratefully into Robbie's chest and let the warm water do its thing, removing smoke and alcohol fumes, washing off mascara and any brave lipstick that managed to survive the three trips to the buffet and six drinks I had.

"I love you. Thank you for the best trip." I lean my chin to his sternum and look up at him.

"You're welcome. Thank you for makin' *every* day the best day."

Do you see why I love this guy?

"I'm not too tired. Wanna go to bed just with you. You an' me, nice and slow this time." Robbie sways with me, hips connecting.

I want that more than anything.

Guess that answers my question. I still have a couple of others, though.

I WAKE UP TO MUFFLED laughter. The bed is empty.

After I sleepily stagger into one of the plush fluffy robes that I am smuggling into my suitcase, I see that a three-handed game of poker has been set up. The giggles are coming from Tess, who has no poker face whatsoever and who occasionally magicks the deck to swap cards around. She *never* does silly stuff with her magic.

I smile. That's a good sign, then. She needs to relax. This is her vacation and it's been intense. A very good kind of intense.

"Lottie! Want me to deal you in?" Robbie opens his arm and I perch on his knee.

"Next hand. What are we going to do inside today?"

Does that sound way more pointedly suggestive, or is it just in my head?

"Matinee show? Magic or music, we can get tickets to pretty much anything," Leo offers.

I let out a silent sigh. Back to normal. No one mentions sexual escapades.

"We can't neglect the hotel pool. They have the big one outside and a smaller one inside. It's a bright, sunny afternoon, so I bet the inside one is mostly deserted," Tess enthuses as she lays down her cards. "I call."

"You gave yourself five aces. Disqualified." Leo rakes the pot of miniature candy bars (where did those come from and why did no one give me any?) to his side of the coffee table.

"I knew I was too excited. Maybe I haven't come down from yesterday yet." Tessa smiles and swipes a Snickers.

Robbie imperceptibly shifts, only letting me feel it as I slip from his knee to his side, waiting for Leo to re-deal. "It was a good night."

There's no sound except the soft slip and slap of plastic-coated cards on the glossy table and Tessa wrinkling wrappers.

"Yeah." I clear my throat. "What happens in Vegas..."

"I- I don't want all of it to stay in Vegas." Tessa meets my eye, her cheeks flushing. "I don't want things that happened here to only happen two thousand miles from home."

"What are you saying?" Robbie asks, shifting again. I see red tint his eyes and fade away fast. He's thinking of the biting and the sexual excitement it caused. I'm thinking of it, too.

We all are.

"You can't go around biting us all the time. It's logistically difficult and leads to major issues with time and exploding porcelain." Leo picks up his cards. "No offense, Charlotte."

"None taken."

"I don't mean all the time! I mean… sometimes. Rarely. Occasionally. We can give each other something when we act together. Together, but separate! Together like we were. Not as in *more* together. With—with parts. No parts."

I have to laugh. "No swinging, Tess. We swear."

"But maybe a little swaying?" she asks hopefully, bottom lip tucked nervously between her teeth as her eyes look into all of ours in turn. By the way she dances over Leo's, and lingers on mine and Robbie's, I can tell they've already talked about it. Robbie and I have sorta-kinda talked about it, too.

"I think some mild swaying with the person we love and the people who love us is okay."

"Okay." Tessa lets out the breath she's holding.

"Right." Robbie also looks like he lost five pounds of tension in his shoulders, smiling in relief.

"Geez, you guys are stressful." Leo suddenly ushers Tessa back toward their room. "Come on, a swim will relax you."

Robbie and I shrug and begin to head off to grab our suits. We hear Leo remark, "And if that doesn't do the trick—we'll just have Lottie and Rob nuke the place."

Robbie growls. I giggle. "They're just jealous, babes. Tessa makes a nice bit of waterworks, but you? You bring the electricity."

"Mm-nn. You make everything feel *so* good," I hiss, hips twitching, pussy tightening experimentally. Yep. Still horny as hell.

Damn.

And yippee.

Robbie inhales and whirls me around as I just barely manage to pull on the bottom half of the bikini I packed. "Robert!" I squeak, using his full name.

He doesn't care if I'm slightly, playfully miffed. His eyes sparkle, tongue tucking behind his teeth in a sudden bad-boy smirk. "We can give 'em a run for their money any day, luv. Wanna show off? They may have the magic, but *we're* the sex gods." His hips roll with mine as his arms go around my waist. "It's in us. It's our gift."

Not a curse. A gift. Maybe everything that's wrong with you isn't that wrong when you have someone who loves everything about you. No matter what he is, I love Robbie. No matter what I can do, he loves me.

I'm glad I'm going to marry this man.

Hell yes, of course, I'm going to show him off.

But I'm going to make us wait a little bit. "Quick visit to the pool, first." I squirm away and into my top.

He groans and snags his trunks.

It's my turn to give him a smirk, a bad-girl smirk that I like to wear, just for him. "A little anticipation goes a long way." I lick the center line of his chest as he straightens up, then swivel from his grasp before he can return the favor.

"Charlotte!"

I escape, laughing as he stumbles into his black trunks as fast as he can.

The good things are worth waiting for.

Tessa and Leo catch me when I fly out. They catch Robbie next. There's a scream, a laugh, and a tumble of swimsuit-covered bodies.

The good things are worth waiting for.

"Best vacation ever." Robbie nuzzles my cheek.

"Best friends, forever."

These are the *best* things and they're worth keeping.

Epilogue

"We've got a tour date! Like, an actual *tour* date!" Robbie slams down his backpack in a gesture of triumph.

I squeal and launch myself out of our tiny little kitchen and pounce on him, leaping, legs locking around his waist as we kiss deeply. "I'm so proud of you, baby!" I gasp. "Where? When?"

"All the NYU campuses and partner campuses! Well, all the ones in New York, anyway. I can't believe it. Leo's over the moon."

"Is that a pun? Oh! The moon! The dates, will they hit the week of the full moon?"

"Thank God, no. It's each weekend in April and May, luv. Be good to have it all sorted before we head off in June."

I blush. A June wedding (an evening wedding, of course) and then two weeks in glorious—Denver. Yeah, Denver. We're not big into sunny beaches right now, can you blame us? But Denver has a ton of snowy, cloudy, artificially generated sun cover, so we're majorly excited. We've got this gorgeous suite in a fancy hotel and... hmm. "Are you sleeping over?"

"Huh? Oh, yeah, on the tour. Doesn't make a lot of sense to drive back from some of the distant ones. I was thinkin' you could come with us." Robbie nuzzles my neck and sighs contentedly.

"Is Tessa going to come with us, too?"

His head darts up, eyes wide. "Do you want us to make this a *special* weekend?"

I nod slowly. We haven't had a "Vegas weekend" since Vegas itself. Sometimes—and this is weird and hot—I know Robbie will take a "sip" of Leo before they get on stage. It amps them both up and I guess it's working. I mean, there are tour dates. Tessa has blushingly told me that she and Leo have replaced their mattress three times since this practice has started. Even magical repairs only work so many times in a row, and it's been a busy season of gigs at little clubs, leading to some bigger clubs, and repeat business at pretty much every club they've played.

"If you don't want to…" I begin, but Robbie shakes his head to silence me.

"I'll text Leo, you text Tess?"

"In a little bit…" I slink my legs down his, but keep my arms wrapped around his neck, pulling him with me into the bedroom.

WE TEXT THEM AFTERWARD, lying naked in our bed, legs crisscrossing over each other as my senses tingle. He licks little traces of me off his lips. "Hit send on three?"

"What'd you write?" I ask.

"'Can Tessa come when we play NYU Albany?' What'd you say?"

"A lot more rambling stuff," I answer quickly and delete half of my tentative text that tried to strike just the right tone. You know, non-pressuring, friendly, fun, hinting, loving—yeah. A lot. I decided to go simple. "Okay, send."

We send.

We get answering beeps in thirty seconds.

"He says yes."

"She says—" I stop and laugh. I love Tess. She's totally my soul-sister. "She says, 'Yes! Oh my gosh, yes! It'll be so much fun. We haven't gotten away in forever. We had a lot of fun last time. Not that this has to be like last time. But yes!'"

After we're done laughing and marveling over the fact that Tessa's brain and my brain are twins (but hers is way smarter and shyer), I arch my back up and slide over to Robbie. "Let me put her mind at ease, and then we're going to have more of our celebratory sex fest."

"Yes, ma'am." He winks.

Slowly crawling up Robbie, I send a reply before I toss my phone to the pillow.

Let's make this like Vegas?

Riding him, my eyes flutter as I see the screen light up. I see Tessa's answer before my eyes close in bliss.

Yes. Encore.

If you enjoyed this tale, I would be so encouraged by a review on Amazon, Goodreads, Barnes&Noble, Bookbub, or any book retailer website or review site.
Thank you in advance, dear readers!

ABOUT THE AUTHOR

BESTSELLING AND AWARD-winning author S.C. Principale believes in writing stories she wants to read, which is why she writes thrillers, mysteries, and steamy paranormal romances. Her stories are filled with strong, sassy heroines and the unique, often otherworldly men who love them. S.C. lives in historic Chester County, Pennsylvania, where haunted battlegrounds serve as never-ending inspiration. S.C. is a self-proclaimed history nerd, following old mysteries, baking, and leading theater and musical groups. Her home life consists of scrounging space for her laptop without tripping over two kids, two dogs, a mischievous chinchilla, and the most patient, sexy husband in the world. **Visit her website for a free gift!** [1]

scprincipaleauthor@gmail.com
Author Website and Newsletter [2]

---

1. https://scprincipale.wixsite.com/website

2. https://scprincipale.wixsite.com/website

[Twitter](https://twitter.com/SCPrincipale)[3]
[Instagram](https://www.instagram.com/s.c.principale/)[4]
[Facebook](https://www.facebook.com/WritesandBites)[5]
[S.C.'s Sultry Sweethearts Facebook Readers Group](https://www.facebook.com/groups/668289727695362)[6]
[Tiktok](https://www.tiktok.com/@scprincipaleauthor)[7]
[Goodreads](https://www.goodreads.com/author/show/14847508.S_C_Principale)[8]
[Amazon](https://www.amazon.com/S.C.-Principale/e/B01FZZL28I%3Fref=dbs_a_mng_rwt_scns_share)[9]

READ THE NEXT PAGE for an excerpt from CrossRealms: Healing Hope by S.C. Principale.

---

3. https://twitter.com/SCPrincipale

4. https://www.instagram.com/s.c.principale/

5. https://www.facebook.com/WritesandBites

6. https://www.facebook.com/groups/668289727695362

7. https://www.tiktok.com/@scprincipaleauthor

8. https://www.goodreads.com/author/show/14847508.S_C_Principale

9. https://www.amazon.com/S.C.-Principale/e/B01FZZL28I%3Fref=dbs_a_mng_rwt_scns_share

SOMETIMES TWO BROKEN people make one whole...

Hope Maguire has always been a loner, both by choice and necessity. She'd learned from a young age not to expect anything from anyone, and that suited her fine. In her line of work, friends would be nothing but liabilities anyway. Most Hunters don't live long, so why get attached? When she's assigned to Malcolm, a stuffy, inexperienced Guardian of the Guild, and then sent to work with the team (ugh!) at the Creek Valley CrossRealms, she's sure it's going to be disastrous.

Self-fulfilling prophecy much?

Approached by a third party and asked to inform on her fellow agents, Hope thinks she's doing the right thing—until it's revealed that she has been a pawn in a deadly double-cross. Now, assassins are after her, and it's run or die. Too bad a near-fatal attack has left her as weak as the prey she used to stalk. Hope knows she is as good as dead. No one will save a Hunter who turned on the good guys. Right?

Malcolm Mansfield-Smythe has always regarded Hunters as tools for killing demons and little else. When his rebellious Hunter betrays them all and then ends up on the chopping block herself, it's tempting to forget about her and keep being the empty, by-the-book man he's always been. Except... he doesn't want to be that hollow automaton anymore, and he doesn't think Hope wants to be a cold-blooded weapon, either. A daring (but poorly planned) rescue leads to a life on the run. Forced to rely only on each other, can two enemies find a way to become friends— or even more?

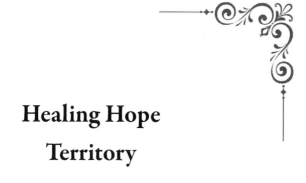

Healing Hope Territory

APRIL 2006

"Winters Interventions." Harold Winters picked up the phone at the front desk. Typically, he remained closeted in the back of the agency, but he was currently short-staffed. This investigative agency, which handled paranormal issues as well as the mundane spousal affairs and stolen property, was simply a cover. Oh, his true work dealt with the supernatural as well, but much more intimately.

Harold Winters was a Guardian of the Guild, the secretive and elite group of men and women who possessed the knowledge to train those who could see through the Mists. The Mists cloud most human eyes to the supernatural elements among them.

His receptionist was one such person, and as such, she was out helping on an assignment, tracking down whatever had been terrorizing a rather rundown area of Creek Valley, home of the California CrossRealms, a place where the Heavenly, Earthly, and Hell Realms were separated by only a thin margin.

"It's me," Beryl, the receptionist in question, chirped cheerfully. "Maddox and I killed a big scaly demon by Scarlet's. He was going to ravish me in the back alley, but then he said that might not be a good idea."

"Who, the demon or Maddox?" Winters felt like he had to double-check. His ravishing receptionist was a reverted succubus, after all. Sex was her second nature, a perk for her lucky human fiancee, the stalwart Maddox.

Beryl made a noise of disgust. "Maddox! I'm not into scales. Plus, Celeste and Auggie are here. Also, it's Friday. We haven't had a nice, demon-free evening in weeks. Well, present company excluded."

"I'll pass on the invitation. We *are* rather slammed at the agency, you know." He loved his agents dearly, despite the clear rules that stated Guardians of the Guild should remain firmly detached from them, especially given their startlingly high mortality rate. "I shall stay here and consult with our recently seconded Guardian."

"You two just want to get rid of all the Americans and then drink all the tea and say words like snog and knickers," Beryl huffed. "I don't like Mansfield-Smythe. He's a pompous ass. Not a *lovable* pompous ass like you are. He says Celeste and Auggie shouldn't work together, and Maddox and I can't have sex on my desk. It's *my* desk!"

"Technically it's my desk as I own the premises and all the furnishings, and I happen to agree with him on that point."

"But Maddox says you'd have a stroke if we used *your* desk."

"I am *not* having this conversation."

"I don't like him. He treats us like robots."

Winters pinched the bridge of his nose to stave off the headache he felt surging forth. For a full decade, he'd worked in Guild Headquarters in London. He oversaw a much larger area with many Guardians reporting to him. He regarded all of them with cool, precise detachment. Only a few years in the Creek Valley CrossRealms with a bunch of young upstarts had turned him soft. Oh, he could assist and train his entire team of young Hunters, Warriors, wiccas, and field agents, even associate with the occasional willing Darkling. But five minutes on the phone with Beryl....

She was still talking about Mansfield-Smythe's many faults. "... never goes on field assignments, wants our reports typed and handed in like we're pupils at some freakshow school, never trains in hand-to-hand with us, never even takes his tie off! I think he irons his underwear. And maybe his hair. If you ask me, it's a waste of a cute face and a nice posh accent."

"I did *not* ask you and he's simply doing what other Guardians do, what *most* other Guardians do. *I* am the aberration, not him. Also, he's quite right to recommend that couples do not work in the field together. It can cause distraction and hinder successful missions and investigations."

"You also have way more at stake and you can't let the baddies win. Look, you're old. You have way more experience than he does. This is his first field assignment, right? You teach him! Don't let him corrupt you."

Winters grimaced against the receiver, "My dear, I'm already considered corrupted and irredeemable by most of the Guild. If Felicia hadn't led this team to victory against the dark forces so many times, they'd have stripped me of my rights and titles, my pension and my salary... even my lapel pin."

"Not the sacred lapel pin." Beryl laughed and turned. A strong hand was kneading her shoulder pointedly. "Saving innocent people makes me horny. Maddox, too."

"Dear Lord."

"Just tell everyone who wants to meet at Scarlet's that we'll be waiting for them. In a dark corner behind some potted plants."

Harold Winters hung up, muttering, "Since when does a crowded hole-in-the-wall club like Scarlet's have potted plants? And I'm not old!" He was only forty-two. Mansfield-Smythe was in his late twenties. He supposed that did seem young to Beryl. "Comparatively speaking."

"Winters?" Felicia Montgomery, Winters' surprisingly petite top agent, poked her head in, a strained smile on her face. "There's some girl here. She says she's a new agent."

"What?" Winters practically fell off of his chair. "New— I haven't asked—"

A leggy brunette sidled in behind Felicia, her siren-red tank top and hip-hugging jeans painted onto her curvy body. "You didn't have to ask, Boss Man. I'm just a gift." She smiled seductively at the open-mouthed Guardian. "It's your lucky day, Mal," she purred, sitting on the edge of his cluttered desk.

Harold practically fainted with relief. "Malcolm! There's a... lady here to see you."

May 2006

"You wanna come with us to Scarlet's?" Felicia tried to make their recent addition, a field agent from the New York area, feel welcome. The entire male population of Creek Valley had certainly done their part.

Hope Maguire gave the smaller, sun-kissed blonde a sex-siren smile, her cherry-black lips parting sensually as she tossed her mane of dark hair. "Nah. Got a hot date."

"I'm surprised Mansfield-Smythe lets you off the lead," Nox was slouched in the back, polishing a lethal-looking blade. He never even looked up, or he would have caught the sudden bitterness on Hope's face. It wasn't a dig at the brunette Hunter, but her stick-in-the-bum Guardian.

Both his barb and his refusal to acknowledge her sex-on-legs posturing rankled more than she'd care to admit. No one owned her. And no way in hell she'd want a pasty, pale vampire, even if he was utterly fuckable, those sharp cheekbones, that accent, those eyes…. Nah. Screw it. Her Warrior senses went haywire whenever she was around him.

"Shut up, Nox. Winters paid you. To use the British slang you love to ruin my ears with, 'shove off.'" Felicia sent a withering glare at the Darkling turned informant-turned-occasional-backup.

No one needed to notice that the glare lingered, meeting his piercing blue eyes for a little too long.

Hope felt a whip crack in the middle of her spine. It was true. What the Rogues said was true.

Nox lifted his head, nostrils flared. Fear? Sex? Adrenaline? He kept his eyes on Felicia. "I'm not invited to Scarlet's, Huntress?"

"You're only here so I don't kill you and because we can't handle Guild business and Winters Interventions business at the same time. Someone must be brewing something." Felicia tore her eyes from his with an effort.

"Yes, so much so that you have to bring in the hired muscle and the slut bomb," Nox chuckled darkly. "And Guardian-the-Younger."

Hope, AKA the slut bomb, drew a stake from her waistband as casually as most would check their phones. "Well, since the slut and the Guardian are here, it seems like they don't need you anymore. I'll just save Winters some money." *And put a stop to what's brewing... Little Miss Innocent can't see the Big Bad Wolf wants to take a bite out of her.*

"Don't!" Felicia pulled Hope's elbow sharply.

"What's wrong, Valley Girl? I'll get you another vamp. One who knows his place." Hope shrugged the smaller woman's arm off, never losing her smile.

"I don't want another vampire! I don't want this one." Felicia felt truth wriggling in the back of her brain. She and Nox weren't friends or anything, but they had a mutual truce. They helped each other. Sometimes... sometimes she thought it might be worth giving her heart to someone again, or at least letting it out of its cage.

"You already had one vamp. That's what everyone says."

"Liam's a decent vampire. He has his human soul. He works for the Guild."

"Ooh, freaky girl." Hope cocked her head appraisingly. "I've heard some Warriors get off on it. The risk. The rush. Maybe I *should* try it myself." Her eyes lingered over Nox's taut body, rising slowly, blade resting on the bench at his back.

"Leave her alone," Nox said in a flat voice, resisting the urge to let his fangs slide free.

Hope's eyes traveled between Felicia and the vampire. Nox didn't have a soul, but he didn't kill. He had some "truce" with Winters and his privileged little pets. All of them were so cuddly close to one another, all "Besties" and "Bros." All bonded. Practically inbred.

Throw in the vampire.

Corruption. Contamination.

"Awww, look at that," Hope breathed. "Got yourself a pet, Montgomery? Is he a good little lapdog? Or more of a pussy?"

A lot of things happened at once. Nox lunged and growled, Hope's stake was raised again, and Felicia jumped in the middle.

"Stop! Nox helps us, he doesn't hurt anyone!" Felicia's fingers locked on Hope's elbows, forcing her raised arms to her sides.

"Mind your mouth," Nox snarled at the struggling brunette.

"I'm surprised she doesn't mind yours. You like the bites, Blondie?" Hope knew she was burning bridges. She didn't care. The Rogues would be in charge soon enough.

There was a crack and a snap. Felicia broke the stake in her bare hand, her Warrior strength on full display. "What the hell is wrong with you?"

"I was just going to ask you the same question. I'm outta here. I'll pass on the drinks. I'm not really into the red stuff," she panted, humiliated. That short little blonde couldn't necessarily beat her, but she could force her to a draw. Hope stormed out.

She was done with those losers.

"YOU WERE RIGHT. YOU guys were so right. They've crossed the line, all of them." Hope paced the gray box-like room.

"The first vampire was a warning. That the Guild ever accepted Montgomery's lover, even with his human soul restored... They wouldn't have if she and Winters weren't so influential. You see how that ended."

"Hot vampires. It's like the gateway drug, man." Hope chuckled grimly.

The shadowy figure continued. "Then the succubi. The witches. There's another vampire among them now, not a soul in sight. He killed several Heaven Fallen in the past, you know."

Hope didn't know, but she nodded as if she did. She never let anyone see a weakness, even a tiny one like ignorance of a simple fact. She'd had a Guardian once. Nice lady. Prim and annoying, rattling on about Mists and magics. She ignored most of it, except for the parts about monsters. She vaguely remembered hearing about Heaven Fallens, too, Warriors and Hunters that had died in battle and been returned to earth with extra powers, way beyond what normal Hunters and Warriors had. So Nox had killed some of them? More to the vamp than she'd thought.

"Nox is more than just an informant from what I've heard. He's bedding Winters' team leader?"

"Miss Perfect? Yeah," Hope lied again, comfortable with lies, far more than the truth. In the weeks that she'd come to be around the little group of agents, she'd come to hate them all. They all... pretended they weren't hurting. They were okay and happy, one big Partridge Family with a side of the undead. Felicia was the worst, a Warrior like her. Blondie clearly wanted to bond... but there was nothing they could bond over. Felicia was living a lie. Warriors and agents don't have friends. They don't have families. They don't have careers and dreams. Felicia still went home to Sunday dinner with her mother, for fuck's sake! She went to college. College.

Like a real girl. Normal girl.

"Maguire, if you don't want this chance, I have a dozen agents more experienced and willing. Let's not forget that you failed to keep your last Guardian alive." The man in the shadows spoke, leaning forward to reveal gray stubble and pulled tight over long jaws.

Hope swallowed hard. That was a low blow, but she deserved it. Her Guardian had been the first one to believe she wasn't some psycho chick, some drug-whore, seeing monsters. She helped Hope to get out of the last mental health facility the state had put her in. They worked together for a little over three months before a demon ripped the middle-aged Guardian in half, right before Hope's horrified eyes.

She was only nineteen when it happened.

She was twenty now, a lifetime in months, barely a year, turning harder than she already was.

I'm an effing diamond.

"I want this chance. Tell me what to do. I'll put that vamp in the ground, you know I can. I've killed—"

"I know you've killed many demons in your short time as a Warrior." The man rose. "I'm sure the Guild has been appropriately grateful?"

Hope hesitated. She ran after her Guardian's body hit the ground, unable to look at the two halves, still twitching. Abandoning her post and turning to her more familiar lifestyle of running, taking, and stealing for survival, the Guild had paid her nothing for the better part of a year. She would have a few weeks' pay soon, now that she'd reluctantly reported to the cardboard cutout, Mansfield-Smythe.

"They're grateful enough," Hope shrugged.

"But we are more so. We are exceedingly grateful to have you as our ally. We can pay you handsomely, take care of you as you deserve to be cared for, an asset, not merely an accessory."

Honeyed words, spoken in a factual voice, a tiny current of the trans-Atlantic running through it. Winters and Mansfield-Smythe had enough toys in their sandbox. She was a lone wolf, meant to stand out. Meant to be feared.

"I'll do it. Anything you say."

"Welcome to the Rogues." The man extended his hand, the rest of his body still bathed in shadow, a key in his palm. "I believe you'll enjoy your new accommodations, a luxury flat. Far better than the slum you've been bunking in."

Hope's cheeks flushed. They knew where she was staying? "Sounds good. What do I call you?"

"Sir."

He rattled her. She never showed that. "Oooh. I could dig it. Strong, silent... shadowy. Strong hands. Strong other things?" Maybe a little spanking, a little choking, a lot of hair-pulling.... She was tired of men who couldn't keep up. She'd guess from his voice that he was in his late fifties, early sixties, way too old for her tastes, but her tastes hadn't always mattered when she needed to trade favors. Powerful, though. Obviously powerful. She liked taking the powerful men to their knees, even if they made her get on hers first. "Why don't you come over here, Baby, and show me?" Sex was a good way to keep them off-balance, too. They thought they were the predators, but oh no. These days, men were always her prey.

"Stop. That sort of talk is detrimental to the cause. There will be no fraternization." The man's voice rang with contempt.

"Sorry. Sir." She hated that word. Both words, actually. Sorry was a word for losers. Well, losers who would admit they were losers. "What's my assignment, Sir? I've infiltrated. Informed."

"You've burnt your bridges there, Maguire. They'll never welcome you back into the fold now."

Hope felt a shiver run through her sinuous body, not the erotic kind she liked. As much as she hated them, Montgomery and her little crew had tried. Mansfield-Smythe was a prick, but he never hurt her.

Aside from the demons, they were good people. Even the demons were pretty harmless.

She could never admit mistakes. Back to that weakness thing. Hope waited in silence for the man to answer her question.

"Winters is being controlled and corrupted. Whether he is aware or not, we can see what's happening, not with that foolish demon-worshipping witchcraft, but with pure science. The energy disturbances are worsening considerably. Soon there will be a Realm Rift, if not a full tear, a total breach. Winters and his team are no longer fit to safeguard this CrossRealms. The Guild itself is not fit. They've been hoodwinked into believing that association with Darklings can be tolerated. It cannot. If they're not stopped, we may lose Creek Valley to the Hell Realm."

Hope swallowed. "That would suck."

He ignored her attempt at understatement. "It's time for new blood to control our efforts in the Mortal Realm. The Guardians are stagnated and weak, misaligned." The English accent grew more pronounced. So did the glint of madness in the gray-blue eyes. "The Rogues must control the California CrossRealms, or we may lose this town, then the state. Demons will flood the realm and spread. We must not be stopped by half-efforts."

"Yes, Sir." This sounded like action. Hardcore, the war is on, guns-a-blazing action. The shiver returned, this time moving lower, resting between her hips.

"Winters' agents are too loyal to him to turn him over to the Guild or to stand down for the Rogues."

"Yeah, I've seen that. It's sick. He's Daddy Dearest to all of them. And that snotty twerp, Mansfield-Smythe, is bad news in a whole different way."

"Precisely. He'll be recalled soon."

"He will?" Hope frowned briefly. How did this guy know the Guild's plans for their prim and proper Poster Boy?

"It's customary to recall the Guardians of a post for debriefing after a tragedy. Once we're in charge, he'll have no need to return"

"What? What tragedy?" Hope shook her head. Had she lost the thread? They were going to prevent the tragedy before it could happen. She hated being called a hero or anything sappy like that, but that was kind of her deal— even if she was pretty bad at it.

"The death of Mr. Harold Winters. I expect him to be removed within the week. I'd appreciate it if you could take out the blonde bitch, too. The wiccas, as well. The succubus and the vampire are a matter of course. The rest are of little consequence."

"But... Winters is a human." Hope cocked her head, stomach churning.

"And?"

"And... I...."

"I don't have time for him to die a natural death. And of course, since you know my desires, I'm afraid I can't really wait for you to die a natural death, either."

Hope jumped at the unmistakable click of a safety going off. "I'll do it."

"Excellent." The man let her see a cold smile for a split second. "Then, when I appoint a new Guardian, I shall place you as his chief agent."

"Guardian?" She cocked her head.

He waved away the slip of a tongue impatiently. "For want of a better term. A Rogue Commander. Now, go. Don't try to contact me. I will contact you. After all," he handed her a piece of paper with an address typed on it, "I know where you live."

Read the next page for an excerpt from: *It's Business, Baby* by S.C. Principale.

It's Business, Baby

Benni Browne never left her house without two essentials— being dressed to slay and having her Bluetooth nestled over her ear, concealed by her perfectly styled hair. Her grandmother, the woman who had raised her and inspired her to push herself every minute of every day, fretted that her thirty-something granddaughter would die before she was forty.

"Baby girl, that thing will give you a brain tumor or the calls themselves are gonna give you a heart attack," Nana G scolded on a weekly basis.

Benni smiled, stepping into her black Mercedes and switching the headset to come through her car's speaker. "Nana, you say that every Friday."

"What else do I say?" her warm, brown sugar voice prompted.

"When am I coming home, when am I going to find a man, and when am I going to have a baby?" Benni checked her sunset red lipstick in the mirror. Perfection. Of course. The president and owner of Body By Browne made sure she was never seen without representing the best of her fashion line. Her taupe heel (bearing the telltale interlinking Bs on the instep) pressed the gas as she reversed out of her parking garage.

"Oh, I don't care so much about the baby, Baby."

They shared a laugh. Nana G was one of the few people Benni bothered to take time to laugh with these days.

"Work-life balance. Dr. Pat on the Hope Network was saying—"

"Nana, Dr. Pat is a quack. You raised me to slay all day, and I do! I have something to tell you." The excitement in Benni's voice told anyone who knew her that she was about to talk business. Pretty much anytime Benni's mouth was open, the comments were either about fashion or business, which went hand-in-hand to her.

"Ooooh, you met someone!"

"No!" Benni swallowed a huff of impatience as she purred past a series of high-rises for the elite, the sky still streaked with stars. Benni didn't believe in pushing anyone harder than she was willing to push herself. That meant she was the first one in the office each morning and the last one out each night. "Nana, this is about the company!"

"Isn't it always?"

Benni ignored that. "I'm getting the cover of *Businesswoman* next month. They did the interview yesterday and the photoshoot next week. They're going to come to the factory and the board meeting... A full four-page spread. The *cover*! Last year, I made the city's Forty Under Forty list. Now, *Businesswoman*. Next? *Forbes* or *Fortune*, Nana!"

Her grandmother crowed with pride and gushed over her success. Benni held each word like a warm blanket, adding layers around her heart. She had to admit, she'd sacrificed a lot to get those accolades. She'd shut out a lot of time-wasters and dropped a lot of friendships that simply wouldn't add to her prestige.

"Okay, Nana, I'm here. I need to get in and get the coffee on." Benni pulled into the parking spot that read: Reserved for Benni Browne, President. She checked her hair and transferred audio back to her headset once again. "I'll come over for dinner next weekend, I promise. I just need to get the spread first. I have a new textile supplier starting, too. It's too crazy this week."

"You always say that. It's too crazy. You're driving that train, Benni! Make it less crazy."

"Hey, this company runs like a well-oiled machine!" Benni beeped the car's alarm and strode into the building, shoulders back in her curve-hugging yellow dress, mocha silk scarf around her waist perfectly accenting her skin color.

In the glassy door's reflection, she grinned, a look somewhere between Cheshire Cat and hunting shark, wide hips and full bust swaying with each step, her body a clock's pendulum. *This is my time.*

"Then when you say it's crazy, that means *you're* the crazy," Nana said sternly. "No one is prouder of you than me, but no one is more worried about you than me, either. Your millions aren't going to keep you warm, your magazine covers aren't going to dry your tears when life gets hard."

"Well, they could. But the ink would run and no one wants that," Benni smothered a laugh. Her grandmother was being serious. A single parent, then a single grandparent, she was probably projecting her own sadness.

"Are you sassing me, young lady?"

"No, ma'am!" Benni swallowed audibly. She could bring a boardroom to their collective knees with one perfectly sculpted eyebrow, but Nana G could torpedo her with a single, dangerous rise in her normally sweet voice. "I know what you mean. I do. I'll keep it in mind and I'll see you next weekend?"

"Talk to you tomorrow morning, Baby Girl. Love you."

"Love you, too."

BENNI MOVED THROUGH her office and set up her morning meetings, started the coffee, and checked the quarterly reports. This week, she had three priorities. One, ensure the talking points in her interview could be backed up by glossy photographs of her design room, the warehouse, her boardroom, and the design floor. Two, get the new textile supplier on the phone and push him off his lazy ass. (She assumed it was lazy, as she'd struggled for months with his predecessor and had been instrumental in getting him terminated after multiple delayed shipments.) Third, make sure the product was going out. That was usually priority number one, but for one week, it could take third place. As an afterthought, she had better make sure to call a department head meeting and explain that this week above all weeks, she didn't need to be bothered with the small shit.

II

"MAVERICK TEXTILES, Marco speaking."

"This is Body By Browne President and Owner Benni Browne speaking." Benni didn't believe in the slow intro. Tell them who you are, then what you want. That's the only way to get ahead, plow through, and don't pick up any deadweight. "We have a shipment of poly silk that's been pushed back three times. I need it by Friday, or I'm cutting your contract."

The man on the other end of the call was silent for a beat. Then, he laughed. Laughed!

No one laughed at Benni Browne unless she told a good joke— and she didn't joke.

"I'm going to need you to do some fast-talking with OPEC and the Shaoxing textile bosses. Call me when you have a shipment of petroleum ready to convert."

Convert? Petroleum? "I have a huge area of my fall line stalled because I need that material," she explained simply. "The world's oil usage is not my problem."

> "Mine, either. I take public transport when I can."
> BEnni stifled a groan. "Do you want this contract, Mr.—"
> "Mercado. Marco Mercado, Head of Maverick Textiles."

Benni swallowed. She knew all of her suppliers, she made a point of it. Suddenly talking to the head honcho didn't unnerve her (nothing unnerved her) but it threw her for a moment. "I usually deal with Mr. Leonard in Supply."

"Mr. Leonard was fired, largely due to your complaints. I told Supply that I will personally handle any calls from Body By Browne."

"Then you can personally handle getting me that product or returning my money and canceling my account with you." She was bluffing. There was no way she would willingly walk away from a supplier this late in the spring, not with a huge chunk of her fall line hanging in the balance.

"You can walk. I'd feel bad for your customers if you did. Every other textile merchant on the eastern seaboard is in the same position. Supply chain snafus and soaring oil prices, not to mention the tense political climate in the Shaoxing textile industry— everyone is hurting for China-sourced materials or polyester products, Ms. Browne."

Benni wasn't unreasonable. She would feel bad for her clients, too. For one thing, Body By Browne was one of the few lines that made daring, sexy clothes for all sizes, particularly the curvy women who still needed to rock a hot mini-dress at the club or kill it in a boardroom-smashing suit. She could see that Marco had valid points. However, she rarely conceded any points that could lead to failure. "But you're working on the problem, aren't you?"

"Of course!"

"Then call me back. I want a status report. *Hourly*. I want that material here by Friday, or I'll cancel your contract, and I'll want my entire deposit back— failure to deliver consumables."

She heard a long, slow whoosh of air. Marco was breathing through his nose. His lips were probably pressed down to a narrow line, jowls wagging with fury. She didn't know what he looked like, but she imagined some fifty-year-old stuffed-shirt barely holding onto his blood pressure because he wasn't used to dealing with a savvy businesswoman who didn't take shit and came equipped with a hefty dose of Black Girl Magic.

"This is the best number to call you on?" Marco answered.

Again, she was off her stride, but she didn't show it. "This is my direct line, yes." It was her business line and her cell. They were one and the same. She had a landline phone at home, but no one but Nana G called her on it.

"Then I'll talk to you at ten. And eleven. And noon. You're going to get sick of my voice, Miss Browne."

"Then you'd better move faster, Mr. Mercado." She snapped a perfectly manicured nail up to her Bluetooth and pressed the button to end the call.

Actually... Mr. Marco Mercado had a nice voice.

As she sat down to start hunting up another textile source on her laptop, her fingers diverted from their mission and typed, Marco Mercado, President of Maverick Textiles. She hit enter and watched her image search explode with photos of a drop-dead gorgeous Latino man in a variety of impeccably cut suits. The tailoring was topped off by sparkling brown eyes and a head of thick, raven-black hair that worked in waves to soften the wide planes of his forehead and chin and accent the knife-like ridges of his cheekbones.

Holy. Fuck.

Mr. Marcado was too damn fine to ignore.

Too bad she didn't believe in socializing with anyone in her business circle. Or anyone at all, period.

Made in the USA
Middletown, DE
27 September 2022